A PACK OF PREDATORS

A PACK OF PREDATORS

A Western Story

S. I. Soper

BLACK STONE
PUBLISHING

Printed in the United States of America

ISBN 978-1-0940-8645-3
Fiction / Westerns

Version 1

CIP data for this book is available
from the Library of Congress

Blackstone Publishing
31 Mistletoe Rd.
Ashland, OR 97520

www.BlackstonePublishing.com

Special thanks to:

*The men and women of the Yuma Prison
Historical Site, Yuma, AZ*

*The Arizona Historical Society, Phoenix, AZ
The Arizona State Parks personnel*

*Without their readily shared historical knowledge,
the description of Yuma Territorial Prison and Jerome
in 1877 would have been merely fabrication.*

—S. I. Soper

PREFACE

Two items of importance occurred in the Arizona Territory in 1876:

On July 1, the Territorial Prison officially opened in Yuma.

In the north between what are now the cities of Prescott and Flagstaff, Al Sieber (who was a scout for General George Crook), Mr. Angus McKinnon, and Mr. M. A. Ruffner, filed copper mining claims at Cleopatra Hill on the eastern slope of Mingus Mountain, where—among other Native Americans—long-vanished Sinagua Indians had for centuries mined extensively and had created several deep "pokes" before they vanished about five hundred years ago.

At the time of this story, Yuma Prison is not quite a year old. The copper-mining town is only a tiny collection of tents and rude wooden shacks not given a name until 1883, but for the sake of clarity, I am calling the site Jerome.

Both Yuma Prison and Jerome played a major part in the history and growth of the American Southwest in general, and Arizona in particular. Today, both sites are historical parks.

CHAPTER ONE

"It rained all night the day I left, the weather, it was dry. The sun so hot, I froze to death, Susanna, don't you cry . . ."

"For the last time, hush your caterwauling, Gibbs! You're drivin' me loco!"

The outlaw slid a grin aside, jerked at the iron manacles tethering him to the saddle, and snapped back: "Well, maybe if you wasn't totin' that body along with us, I wouldn't have to try to keep my mind off the fact that I got a corpse on my tail. Why the hell couldn't you just give Larson a decent buryin' and leave him be, Marshal? Why you got to cart the poor bugger all over the damned countryside?"

Buck Fyffe jammed a thumb up under his hat brim to push it back and let what little breeze there was cool his forehead. Late afternoon here in the low desert was ungodly hot, but the temperature was the least of his worries. Hair on the back of his neck prickled with more than sweat. Now that his deputy, Steve Larson, was dead, he was alone with Luther Gibbs, and he wanted to stay that way. If Gibbs's men were somewhere out there in the brush planning to rescue their leader from him before he could get Luther to Yuma Territorial Prison, he wanted to be able to hear them coming, and he couldn't do that with Gibbs singing at the top of his lungs.

"I know, I know, you tol' me," Luther went on. "Poor ol' Larson was your friend. Couldn't just drop him in a hole in the ground and forget him. Gotta take him home to his wife and kids. Hell, no deputy marshal oughtta be married anyhow, as I see it."

"Shut up, Gibbs!"

"As I see it, any woman who marries a lawman is a widow in the makin'. You got yourself a woman, Marshal Fyffe?"

"No, and if you don't stop yammering, I'm goin' to yank your boot off and stuff it in your damned mouth!"

Gibbs laughed. "Aw, now, you wouldn't do a thing like that, Marshal. Not you. You got a reputation to uphold!" Gibbs's eyes ranged over a desert thick with greasewood, creosote bushes, and, here and there, cholla cacti. The occasional elegant saguaro thrust arms skyward over elf owls nesting in holes previously occupied by Gila woodpeckers; come evening, they would hunt on small, silent wings, but at the moment they hid from the late-June heat.

He went on. "Babyface Buckley Fyffe always gets his man, but he's damned upfront and straightforward about it. An honest man! By the book, they say! Nothin' mean about ol' Buck Fyffe, they say. Any mis-cre-ant is plumb lucky to be took by Marshal Buckley Fyffe, I'll have you know!

"Well, you're provin' it, I'll tell you, cartin' your poor dead pardner all over creation. I never saw a man die so quick from a sidewinder's bite! Must have got a tooth right in a vein. Usually takes upward of a half-hour or more, y'know, if ever, but not poooor ol' Larson. Less than fifteen and he was gone. Right in a vein, I'll wager.

"Well, at least I won't have to lissen to him coughin' all day and night, now. I swear, he was dyin' of the lung fever, anyhow. Prob'ly was a blessin' he went quick the way he did."

"That does it." Buck reined his mount in sharply and pulled the lead rope to move Gibbs's horse close. Larson's black gelding, with the deputy's blanket-wrapped body securely bound to the saddle, halted behind them.

Luther lost his grin. He began: "Now, Marsha . . ."

"Shut your trap!" Buck reached over and yanked the bandanna from Gibbs's neck. "I told you and told you, now I'm gonna have quiet, dammit!" The cloth wadded in his left hand, he drew his sidearm with his right and thumbed the hammer. "That biscuit hole has been flappin' for a hundred miles, so open it now or I'll open it for you."

Luther looked at the blue eyes cold in the clean-shaven face, and his own went as hard. He snarled: "Why don't you grow a mustache and beard so you'll at least look like a man, Fyffe. I take offense at bein' escorted to Yuma by a snot-nosed kid!"

"I'm thirty-five, Gibbs, but even if I was fifteen, I could still handle the likes of you. Open your mouth!"

Gibbs leaned away from him as far as the manacles and the rope that ran from ankle-to-ankle under the horse's belly allowed. "You ain't gonna stuff that in my . . ."

"The hell I'm not!" Fyffe aimed the pistol. "I could gun you down with impunity, as they say. Tell 'em you were tryin' to escape. You push me one hair more, and I'm going to do it. I've had it with you, Luther. You seem to think that the twenty-five thousand dollars you stole from Southwestern will still be waitin' on you fifteen years from now and that makes you a big man in outlaw legends, but I tell you, it doesn't cut the mustard with me. Now, you goin' to open up, or are you goin' to lose your front teeth?"

Gibbs bared the teeth in question before he concluded that the marshal was serious and opened his mouth. Buck jammed the wad into the space and waggled his weapon in warning. "You spit that out, Luther, you're in more trouble than you ever dreamed of." He leathered his pistol, cast a careful eye around the desert, and nudged his horse back into motion. For the next hour, the only sounds were the wind clashing creosote branches, the horses' hoofs, and an occasional hawk crying from far above.

At sunset, Buck led his miniature cavalcade to a copse of tamarisk on the edge of a deep arroyo and dismounted stiffly. He untied one end of the ankle rope, unlocked Gibbs's manacle chain from the saddlebow, and helped the outlaw down. Gibbs stumbled and went to his knees. Buck jerked him upright, manhandled him toward a spot of barren sand, and dropped him.

Gibbs didn't resist, but glared hotly. He made unintelligible noises from behind the gag before he eased back to lay propped on an elbow and watch while Buck loosened cinches but didn't unsaddle the animals, then picked the canvas water bag from Larson's mount. Fyffe drank from the bag first. His light-brown hair was stringy and dark with sweat when he took off his hat, set it upside down on the ground, filled the crown, and watered his gelding. He repeated the process with Gibbs's and Larson's horses, jammed the wet hat back over his hair, and turned to Luther.

"Now you can spit, Gibbs."

Luther took a deep breath and blew wadded cloth out of his mouth. He drank greedily when Buck shoved the water bag neck at him; then again lay back to watch Fyffe build a small fire and start dinner. They ate silently—canned beans, fatback, an apple each, and coffee.

"Y'know," the outlaw murmured over his cup, "you're nothin' but a delivery boy. I been watchin' you, Marshal. You got a title, yeah . . . you is Federal Marshal Buckley Fyffe, lawman. Sounds nice, but what you got to go with it? You have a fine house somewhere, eh? You have a soft bed waitin' on you to get back to it, with a pretty lady smellin' of lavender to warm it with you, eh? How much you make, wage-wise, tell me that, Marshal?"

Buck glanced at Luther, but said nothing. He was tense. Their superior, Lon Humbert, had sent him and Steve out together to back each other up on the trip down the mountain from Prescott to Yuma so one could stand watch over Gibbs while the other slept. There had always been one of them alert and on guard. But because of Larson's unexpected death, he was now alone with Luther. It was another two-and-a-half to three days—and nights—to the prison. Could he stay awake two or three days and nights straight?

Gibbs slurped noisily at his coffee cup before he went on. "Now, me, I got twenty-five thousand dollars hid out there, and only I know where. Not even my men know where my cache is, and you know I didn't tell 'em up in Prescott. So now, let's you and me dicker here. How much did you say you made in wages?"

"I didn't," Buck said shortly.

"Embarrassed about what a piddlin' sum you pull in? Well, let me offer you . . . oh, let's say . . . a thousand bucks. I'll guide you to my money . . . you take a thousand and I'll take the rest. You go off to . . . let's say, San Francisco or some big fancy town back East. You vanish with your take, as it were, I disappear with mine, and we'll both be happy."

"Luther." Buck dumped coffee dregs to the sand and stood. "You're tryin' to bribe a law officer. That could add to your jail time. I tell you, you run off at the mouth more than any man I ever met . . . You want me to gag you again?"

"Hey!" Gibbs lifted chained arms in mock defeat. "I ain't

tryin' to bribe you, Babyface Fyffe, I'm puttin' forth a legitimate business proposition! Uh . . . a thousand don't interest you, how 'bout . . . five or ten? You say you're thirty-five. Okay, you're thirty-five. Been marshalin' for the last eight or ten years, eh? What have you got to show for it, tell me that. Think of what you could do with five or ten thousand dollars, sir."

Buck let the man talk and began scouring tin plates with sand. He flashed a quick look around. It was dark out there now, the vast spaces made even denser by the tiny circle of light cast by his little campfire. He shut Gibbs's voice out and listened for other sounds. Nighthawks. Over there, a kit fox yapped. Elf owls warbled like gloomy doves. Abruptly, a coyote sang to the early stars and was answered by two or three far voices. Only the natural creatures.

He wiped residual grit from the plates with the heel of his palm and had just turned to store them in his saddlebags when faint sounds other than normal wildlife brought him around with his pistol in his hand. Luther, the rope trailing from one ankle and manacles notwithstanding, was headed into the blackness at the edge of the clearing.

Buck aimed and pulled the trigger. Gibbs howled as he plunged to the ground. Fyffe jammed his gun back into his holster and strode across the clearing. Blood stained the side of the outlaw's soiled blue shirt when Buck hoisted Luther upright, dragged him back to the campfire, and dropped him.

"That was a stupid thing to try, Luther. Where did you think you were goin' in the dark and in chains?"

"You shot me!" Gibbs gritted. "I'm bleedin' like a stuck pig! Damn you, Fyffe, you sonovabitch, you could have run me down! You din't have to shoot me!"

Buck bent over the man and pulled the shirttail out from under the belt to lift bullet-perforated cloth away from the wound. "I only grazed you, Luther. That's nothin' but a scrape." He wadded the cloth and pressed it against the gouge before he shoved the man down flat, wound the rope tightly around Gibbs's legs, and tied it off. "Go to sleep. We got a long day ahead of us tomorrow."

Clutching his ribs, Luther smirked. The sound of Fyffe's gunshot had rolled off across the desert in all directions, and if his men were out there looking for him . . .

He murmured: "Yessir, Marshal Fyffe . . . yessir, sir. I'll do jus' that." He closed his eyes. "Oh, Susanna, don't you cry for me . . ."

"Good." Buck grinned. "Keep it up, Luther. Your off-key croakin' will be sure to keep me awake. You won't get another chance to snake away on me."

"Shit," Gibbs breathed, and shut up on his own.

* * * * *

Three off-riders also halted for the night. They built no fire to betray their presence. After dark, while two stayed with the horses, one crept near enough to get a clear view of Fyffe's camp. He was relieved at midnight by a fresh eye to continue the surveillance. In the morning, the three continued to follow at a discreet distance.

* * * * *

Buck was scratchy eyed and saddle sore, and it was not yet noon. He knew what Luther Gibbs tried to do yesterday by singing at the top of his lungs, and then with that half-assed escape attempt into the night. Gibbs thought his men were scouring the desert to locate and rescue him before the law could get him to Yuma Prison, and hoped his bellowing and the gunshot would lead them to him.

In a way, the marshal had played into Luther's hands by firing his weapon at the man instead of running him down, snagging him, and hauling him back to the campfire. In another, he felt he'd had little choice. Chains or not, Gibbs was as big a man as he was—in fact, they owned about the same build—armored with thick metal manacles, and was meaner than sour swill. If he had let Luther find a hiding place in the brush and had given him the opportunity to leap out and bash him with those chains, he could have been in more trouble than he was in now.

And he was in trouble. He had no doubt that Gibbs's men were out there looking for their leader, which was why he and Steve had cut cross-country instead of sticking to the wagon road between Prescott and Ehrenberg on the Colorado, then riding on down to Yuma. The court hadn't wanted to waste the iron tumbril on just one prisoner who, as far as anyone knew, had never murdered anyone and wasn't considered to be that dangerous, so Lon Humbert had commissioned Larson and him to escort Gibbs to Yuma. Five men in Gibbs's gang to two law officers hadn't been such bad odds, but now that Steve was dead, five to one—six, if you counted Gibbs—wasn't healthy. And whether or not Luther's cronies felt any special loyalty or held any real fondness for the man himself, it seemed that their leader had stashed Southwestern's cash in some spot only he knew. Without Luther, his men didn't get their share of the twenty-five thousand. That was enough to buy many a hard-case's allegiance.

He rubbed his eyes before he glanced over at his prisoner to make sure Gibbs was still secure, then back at Larson's blanket-shrouded body. How was he going to tell Rose she was a widow? God, how could he do that? Steve and Rose Larson had sort of taken him in after his wife Laurie and their baby had died of the fever. They'd had him over for dinner whenever he was in town, and Rose had even tried to fix him up with her sister, Mavis. They were more than friends, almost family, and to have to tell Rosie . . .

Well, surely Yuma had an undertaker. He would get Steve a decent casket, buy a wagon, and . . .

"Marshal, you intend to stop for lunch or are we gonna just ride on forever, here?"

Luther's question jerked Buck out of his line of thought. He hadn't gotten much sleep. Trying to keep an eye on Gibbs and their surroundings while alone didn't lend itself to a restful night. He had drifted off once, lulled by the silent dark, the crackle of his small fire, and Luther sawing wood a few feet from him, only to awaken with a start to discover Gibbs in the act of reaching for the carbine he held across his knees. After that, he drank a lot of coffee. Tonight, because he was already so tired, he would have to set his principles aside, tether Luther to something sturdy, and chance resting, for a while at least.

He picked a thicket with a little shade, led Gibbs's and Larson's horses to it, dismounted and ground-tethered the animals. When he untied the water bag from Steve's horse and started to pour water into his hat crown for his own mount, Gibbs snarled: "For gawd's sake, untie me, Marshal! I gotta go do my business here!"

Buck subdued the urge to let the outlaw merely mess his pants, nodded, set the water bag and his hat on the ground, and stepped up to untie the rope from Luther's ankles. That done, he dug the key out of his watch pocket, unlocked Gibbs from the saddlebow, replaced the key, and moved away, a palm on his gun butt.

Luther grinned. He sang: "Ohhhh . . . I came to Ala-bama

with my ban-jo on my knee, but I'm goin' to Yooo-ma prison, 'cause I'm no longer free!"

Buck's eyes widened to a flash on intuition. He had the side-arm half drawn before the business end of a lariat settled over his head. The loop tightened around his throat and nearly broke his neck when he was jerked backward. The weapon skittered from his fingers as he hit the ground; he grabbed at the rope with both hands, because he was being dragged across the dirt.

Abruptly, men and horses were all around him. The noose shut off his breath; he struggled more again to reach the rope than against the hands that yanked his arms down, but then Luther bellowed: "Ease up, Jake! I want the pleasure of killin' that bastard myself!"

* * * * *

Out among the cacti and creosote, the off-riders grinned silently at each other and nodded. They dismounted and again watched through binoculars. They didn't interfere, because things were taking a turn for the better over there.

CHAPTER TWO

The moment the outlaw named Jake Lambert eased the rope and black spots stopped dancing in front of his eyes, Buck renewed his fight against the hands that held him. He got one arm free. His fist in a man's teeth skinned his knuckles, but two men replaced the one he had knocked aside, and they again immobilized him.

On his back in the dirt, with three hardcases holding down his arms and a fourth across his legs, and Jake, astride his horse, keeping the rope taut but not completely choking him, Buck looked with everyone else at Luther.

Grinning broadly, Gibbs moved to where Fyffe's weapon lay in the dirt and picked it up. The outlaw leader took a moment to untie the rope trailing from his right ankle before he sauntered to where Buck lay, straddled the marshal's body, and sat down on Fyffe's pelvis.

Gibbs pressed the end of the pistol barrel up under Fyffe's nose before he said: "Took you boys damned long enough to get here."

"Hey, boss," one growled, "it's a big desert. We did the best we could."

"Yeah, well, better late than never. Now . . ." He leaned toward Buck, watching him silently before he said: "Babyface, you're about to lose your young good looks."

Buck's eyes narrowed. He swallowed to make sure his voice would work, slipped another look at the men holding him down, and said past set teeth: "You kill me, Gibbs, every lawman in the territory will be houndin' you for the rest of your life. You'll never get a moment's peace. Wherever you put it, that twenty-five thousand will molder away for lack of spendin'."

"Well, now, Babyface, that's my problem, not yours, ain't it?" Luther thumbed the hammer. "But then, you won't be around to . . ." His words stopped when his brows lifted. "Oh, well, wait a minute, here! Oh, now, you just gave me an idea!" His men scowled at him when he eased the hammer, raised the weapon, and hoisted himself off Fyffe's belly.

Gun still in hand, Gibbs snapped the manacle chain between his wrists. "Ol' Judge Hauser had a message sent from Prescott down to Yuma tellin' the superintendent there that Babyface, here, and poooor ol' dead Larson, facedown over that horse, there, was bringin' me in for a fifteen-year stretch, so they are expectin' ol' Luther Gibbs to be a guest shortly, right?"

Jake dismounted but still held the end of the lariat looped around Buck's neck. He frowned. "What you gettin' at, boss?"

Luther scratched his chin with the forward sight on the pistol barrel. "Ol' Buck here said it. I don't show up to take residence, the law is gonna be lookin' for me . . . by association, you boys, too. But if Marshal Buckley Fyffe and Deputy Marshal Steve Larson bring Luther Gibbs in and turn him over all legal and proper, that's the end of it, right? Oh, I expect the authorities will try to get Gibbs to disclose the money's hidin' place from time to time, but, hell, I don't tell 'em . . . the money's safe, right?"

"You been out in the sun too long, boss," one of the others began. "I mean, after all the time we spent lookin' for you . . . Uh . . . we rescued you here, boss, but now you . . ."

That sinking feeling in Buck's gut went even colder when Luther laughed.

"You got no imagination, Fisher, which is why I'm primo here and you ain't." Gibbs waved the pistol at Fyffe. "He keeps the key to these chains in his watch pocket. Ed, get it out and unlock me, would ya? Then, we're goin' to have us some fun. And we'll get the law off our trail in the process!"

With men holding him down and another keeping the noose secure around his neck, Buck could do nothing to stop the one called Fisher from picking the key out of his pocket and unencumbering Gibbs. He lay on the hot dirt and breathed carefully, half curious as to what Luther had in mind, three-quarters furious for allowing himself to fall into the outlaws' hands. Why hadn't he heard their approach? Well, maybe they hadn't approached; perhaps they had lay in wait for him. If so, he'd stopped right where they'd wanted him to, hadn't he?

Fisher flung the manacles aside but kept the key. Luther put the pistol down, stepped to where Buck's hat sat, picked it up, slapped dirt from it, and settled it on his head. Grinning, he ran a finger around the brim to adjust its slant before he nodded to his men and said: "Up him."

Hands hauled Fyffe to his feet.

Gibbs nodded. "Stand back, men, but keep him covered. Jake, hang on to that rope around his neck. Now, Marshal Babyface, take off your clothes. All of 'em."

Buck thought to ask Gibbs what he had in mind, but figured maybe he didn't want to know. The others released him and moved a few feet away; though they weren't holding him now, he was solidly surrounded. The sound of hammers cocked on four drawn weapons was dull in the noon heat, but pointed. He gritted teeth and slowly reached for his gun-belt buckle.

Simultaneously, Luther began unbuttoning his own shirt. When Buck stood in only his underwear and socks and was reaching for those, Gibbs said: "No, no, that's enough. Move him back, Jake, and let's see what we got here."

Fyffe grabbed at the noose with both hands and got fingers under it when—if he remembered Gibbs's men's names rightly—Jake Lambert yanked the rope. He stumbled backward away from the pile of clothes and cast a quick look at the others. Though they watched Luther, their weapons didn't waver.

Gibbs, himself in his underwear and Buck's hat, the bullet scrape along his ribs blackly scabbed, picked up the sweat-stained gray shirt and shook dust from it. He put it on, followed it with the black pants and gun belt. He fingered the marshal's badge pinned to the front before he shrugged into the black vest. He pulled the leather wallet containing Fyffe's credentials from the back pants pocket, opened it, shuffled papers until he located the incarceration order for Luther Ben Gibbs, bank robber, train robber, stagecoach holdup man, and general lowlife, scanned the papers, grinned in satisfaction, and returned them to the folder. He stuffed the wallet back into his pocket and waved a finger at Fyffe, who was still watching him silently.

"Ease up on the rope so he can get dressed, Jake." He reached for Fyffe's boots and jammed a foot into one. "We wouldn't want our friend to get sunburnt."

Warily, Buck bent for Gibbs's clothing. He had the pants and shirt on and was in the process of tucking in the shirttail, when Luther grunted: "Huh! Details. Gotta watch the details. Hold up, Babyface. Cover 'im, boys." Gibbs scooped up the manacles, and grinning like a rabid coyote, tossed them to Fisher. "You still got the key, Ed. Lock him up tight."

Now, Buck knew what Gibbs was doing. He stepped back to further loosen the noose around his neck, thrust the rope up and over his head, flung it aside, and, despite all the weapons pointed at him, crouched slightly. "You'll never get away with it, Gibbs. I've been around a long time. I know people all over the territory, and they know me. You can't pass yourself off as me for long. You're bound to meet somebody who . . ."

"Don't shoot him, men," Luther interrupted, "but take him!"

Fyffe's fist sent Moses Little to the ground with a spurting nose, and his elbow in Cecil Clapp's solar plexus doubled the owlhoot, but Jake Lambert, Blue Paley, and Ed Fisher pounced on him. They held him struggling and swearing long enough for the other two to recover.

Little sprang back into the group. Knuckles flashed golden lights inside Fyffe's head when Moses hit him. A second blow weakened his knees. The men got him down again and held him while Luther used the manacles to lock his wrists in front of him.

Panting heavily, Buck squeezed eyes back into focus in time to see Gibbs bend to pick up his pistol from the ground. The outlaw leader blew dirt from the weapon, checked the load, sighted down the inner barrel to ensure it was clean, and nodded.

"Now," Luther said, "details. Cecil, lemme borrow your pigsticker for a minute." Clapp loosened fingers from Fyffe's shirt collar long enough to pull the big Bowie-style blade and hand it, hilt-first, to his leader. Gibbs said: "Thank you, Cec. Up him."

Once again, the men lifted Buck to his feet. Fyffe stiffened in their hold when Luther waggled the knife at him. "Details." Gibbs grinned again. "You're wearin' a bullet-ventilated shirt, Babyface, complete with dried blood. But no wound, right? It'd be a little detail like that that'd send us to wrack and ruin, so . . ." He inserted the blade into the nearest bullet hole in the fabric until the point met flesh, then pressed to make a cut in the skin. "Pull up his shirt, Blue, and hold it, but get out of the way. I wouldn't want to plug you accidental. And you, Babyface, I'd say it's in your best interests to hold real still now."

A forearm over his throat, fingers in his hair, and hands holding his elbows out to each side to stretch the wrist chain across his chest kept Buck immobilized while Luther aimed at the knife nick and pulled the trigger. Fyffe choked a harsh cry of pain when the bullet skidded along a rib. Abruptly, he was on hands and knees at the outlaws' feet while they chuckled around him. Blood soaked the shirt again and pooled over his belt when he got up on his own this time and stood glaring at Luther while the outlaw leader nodded.

Now, there was no humor in the Luther Gibbs snarl. "Details. You say your face is well-known, Marshal? We got what . . . two or three more days, if we dilly-dally, till we get to Yuma? By the time you get there, Babyface, nobody's gonna recognize you, and maybe we'll just ruin your reputation as a fine, straight-shootin', upstandin' lawman to boot."

He nodded to Moses. "Little, over on the black is the deputy marshal's body. If I recollect rightly, Fyffe here took Larson's papers and his badge and all off the corpse before he bundled it up. You and Blue look through his pockets to make sure we don't miss somethin' important, then dump Larson's body under any ol' handy bush. I ain't haulin' no corpse all over the desert, I'll tell you that!

"Then, Cec, get Larson's other clothes out of his saddlebags and put 'em on. I think they'll fit you. And his badge and papers. You are now Steve Larson, Deputy US Marshal!

"Ed . . . Jake . . . keep a close eye on our friend, there. After all, we got to get Luther Gibbs to Yuma!"

Outraged, Buck watched the outlaws cut the corpse from the saddle, slide it to the ground, loosen ties that secured the blanket-like shroud, and search Larson's pockets. His side burned from the bullet wound. He was in chains and held by one man, with a second behind him poking a pistol into his spine, and was helpless to stop it.

Blue Paley said: "Ain't nothin' on him, boss."

Luther nodded. "Then fling some brush over him and be done with it."

Fyffe grated: "Dammit, Gibbs, at least bury him properly! Don't just let Steve lay! The coyotes, foxes, and javelinas will get at him! For God's sake, man . . ."

"He's dead," Luther shot back. "Nothin' but a shell. He don't care what happens to him now."

Buck wrenched against the hands holding him. "I care, Gibbs! He was my partner . . . my friend! Let me loose and I'll dig his gr—"

Gibbs leaped at him. Knuckles caught him hard in the mouth and staggered him into Jake Lambert behind him. Luther snapped: "Ol' Steve wasn't my friend, Fyffe, and you shut up or I'll gag you like you done me!"

Cecil Clapp had been searching Larson's saddlebags and bedroll and had come up with Steve's fringed leather vest. He located Larson's credentials folder and badge, shoved the wallet into his back pocket, pinned on the star, donned the vest, flung his hands wide to strike a pose, and everyone but Buck laughed when he drawled: "Well, whaddya know 'bout that! I'm a li'l ol' lawman."

Luther nodded. He said: "All right, men, let's find a more comfortable spot to spend the night. You all, put Fyffe on the bronc I was ridin', and I'll take his horse. Ed, be sure to lock that bastard down tight to the saddle. There's the ankle rope. And Cecil, you might as well ride Larson's black. It still has all his stuff there. Jake, you bring Cec's horse."

Then, he chuckled. "In a couple of days, I, Marshal Buckley Fyffe, and ol' Cecil, there, as Deputy Marshal Steve Larson, are gonna deliver Luther Ben Gibbs to Yuma Territorial Prison, as is our bounden duty. Then, men, we're free to spend our booty anywhere and any way we want without the law on our tails!"

They forced Buck to the horse, heaved him aboard, secured the wrist chain to the saddlebow, ran the rope from ankle to ankle under the animal's belly, cinched it securely, and leaped astride their own mounts. Surrounded by laughing, jostling outlaws, Fyffe looked back once at Steve's corpse lying on the sand, his pockets turned inside-out and only a token branch across his chest. High above, two black dots already marred the sky, vultures called to a prepared meal.

He jerked his eyes away. He would never tell Rose. He would say that he had put her husband in a desert grave, unmarked but decent. No, he would never betray that Steve had been left lying exposed to scavengers. He knew she couldn't handle that, because he barely could.

The sun hot on his bare head, he squinted into shimmering southern spaces and stiffened his spine. Two and a half or three days between here and Yuma. He had not yet been to the territorial prison. It was new, had opened only a year ago in 1876, and though it wasn't yet completed, it had already gained a reputation as a hellhole. At the moment, he didn't know if there was anyone on the prison staff that he knew or who would recognize him, but there might be, because as he'd said to Gibbs, he'd been around a long time.

That thought brought greater tension. He had been a lawman for a long time—almost eleven years. Abruptly, he wondered how many inmates incarcerated in the new prison were those he had captured, and if he couldn't somehow get out of this mess and actually ended up inside Yuma, how many of those men would recognize him?

Teeth clenched until jaw muscles ached, he applied himself to survival. Daylight wasn't what worried him—his outlaw escort now rode hard and fast and mostly in silence, leading his horse and Cecil's mount riderless since Clapp had taken over Steve Larson's. What brought a cold clutch to his heart was thought of this evening around the campfire, because the occasional look Gibbs cast his way and the following chuckles out of the owlhoot told him that Luther worked overtime on some sort of scheme, and he knew he wouldn't like what Gibbs had in mind.

What with his lack of sleep last night, his battle with Gibbs and his men today, and the tension of pondering his desperate situation and shadowed future, Buck was exhausted by the time Luther pointed to a thick copse of tamarisk and cactus ahead. "There's the Well. We'll camp there. Tomorrow night, we'll be at Cañon Springs. Then, it's only 'bout fifty miles on to Yuma." The outlaw shot a grin at Buck. "Gettin' closer to your just desserts, Mistuh Gibbs. Won't be long, now."

Buck met Luther's eyes briefly. He said nothing.

* * * * *

Out in the brush, the off-riders raised brows to each other, because things were growing more and more interesting by the moment over there to the east. They could hardly wait to see what came next. They continued to follow.

CHAPTER THREE

Falling stars scraped silver lines across an indigo sky. Silent-winged elf owls pursued prey among bats whose miniature size rivaled their own, and an occasional great horned owl was a diabolical shadow against the moon. Nighthawks cut the air with scythe-like wings. Somewhere close by, a herd of javelinas, stinking of musk and sparse hair bristling, faced down a cougar and confiscated a deer carcass. There was nothing quiet or benign about the desert, either in the baked earth–scented air or on the sand, for night was a killing time populated by predators hidden from the heat of day.

Buck stood in the circle of firelight, his wrists still manacled in front of him. The rope that bound his ankles beneath the horse's belly had been shortened to some twelve inches so he could shuffle along, but not run. He frowned warily at Luther when Gibbs noted: "You look like death warmed over, Fyffe. I think you're comin' along fine. But let's us chat here for a while. I'd like to know my . . . shall we say . . . other self." He chuckled into his coffee when he sipped before leaning back onto an elbow, the tin cup in both hands. "Where you from, originally, boy?"

"Virginia. Near Winchester."

"Ah-ha. As I recollect, you said you're thirty-five. You in the War Between the States?"

Buck looked right and left. The outlaws sat, squatted, or reclined in a ring around him, their expressions curious but not particularly menacing at the moment, but he knew that could change instantly. He said: "No."

"No!" Luther's brows rose. "I'm surprised! I would've thought a fine, upstandin' critter like you would have fought on one side or t'other as a matter of principle. How come you din't?"

Fyffe's expression turned grimmer for a moment. He again studied his captors briefly before he said: "I was the youngest of five boys. My father was an abolitionist. He and my oldest brother were killed when we helped Osawatomie Brown raid the government arsenal at Harpers Ferry in '59. One of my brothers was captured then. My other two brothers and I escaped along with a couple other men, and . . ."

Gibbs's mouth fell open to amazement before he blurted, "You knew ol' John Brown personal? Well! First time I ever met somebody who knew Brown personal! How old were you then?"

"Seventeen."

"So you were . . . uh . . . nineteen when the war broke out? Prime bullet-fodder! What? . . . You see enough killin' with ol' John Brown? That why you din't join one side or t'other?"

"Not entirely. My family owned a farm. Our mother was elderly. She would have been alone had we all left to fight. My two older living brothers joined the North, but they made me promise to stay and look after Mother."

"Humph." Luther Gibbs finished his coffee and tossed the cup toward the fire. "So, since you din't get any action durin' the war, after it was over and your brothers got home, you decided to move west and make your own excitement?"

"Neither of my brothers came back."

"Oh, well, now!" Luther made an insincere sound of sympathy. "Husband and four sons lost to the war! That must have been real hard on your poor ol' ma! How come you deserted her, too, I ask ya?"

"Mother died December 30th of '64. The war was over before I could get there."

Again, Gibbs grunted: "Humph." He added: "So, how long you been a lawman?"

"Since '66." Buck knew the why of all these questions; if Luther intended to impersonate him, the man needed to know as much about him as possible. He could have lied, but figured it wasn't worth the effort. What was worthwhile was finding a way out of this mess, and while his mouth automatically answered, his mind searched for some means of escape. He hoped that if he cooperated, he could lull the outlaws into carelessness, and then he would be gone.

Gibbs asked: "And in all that time, you never got yourself a steady woman?"

"Yes, I had a wife and a daughter. Laurie and the baby died of typhoid."

"But not you."

"I . . . wasn't there at the time." And it still hurt. That he had been away tracking outlaws at the moment his wife and child had needed him most continued to drive a spike into his heart.

"Well, that's the way of it, I guess," Luther nodded. "Now . . ."

"Whoa," Buck interrupted. "I answered your questions, Gibbs, now I have one for you." He nodded around the circle of outlaws. "These are your men, right?"

"Yup." His expression smug, Luther settled back onto both elbows.

"They've been ridin' hell-bent all over this desert lookin' to rescue you, right?"

Now, Gibbs's brows lowered over cool blue eyes. "What you gettin' at, boy?"

Buck shrugged. "Seems they're real loyal to you. How come you don't trust them enough to tell them where you hid Southwestern's twenty-five thousand dollar take?"

Gibbs sat up. He scowled. "That wasn't planned! We got separated, and I just happened to have the money, that's all."

"Ah! Fine! But now that you're back together, don't you think it would be a show of good faith on your part if you let them in on the hiding place?"

Buck was rewarded by mutters of agreement and abruptly resentful looks around the circle of men.

Gibbs snapped: "I'm not goin' to run off at the mouth with you lissenin', Fyffe!"

Chain links clinked when Buck flourished his hands. "So, I'll leave. No problem, there."

"Oh no you don't!" Luther frowned. "I see what you're tryin' to do, Babyface, and it's not goin' to work. You take us all for idjits?"

"Not you, Luther," Buck said quietly. "But let me tell your men what else I see comin' over the horizon. You and Cecil haul me on into Yuma Prison, you as me and Cecil as Steve. You bamboozle the warden into thinkin' you're me. You establish that you're me. Then, as Marshal Buckley Fyffe and Deputy Larson, you two go out and bring in most of the rest of the Luther Gibbs gang. Now, we have twenty-five thousand divided by two instead of six, and . . ."

"Shut up, Fyffe," Gibbs snarled.

Buck hurried on. ". . . then, you'd know no lawman will be chasin' the Gibbs gang!" He flashed a quick look at Clapp. "If I were you, Cecil, I'd sure as hell watch my ba—"

Gibbs sprang upright and at him. Buck ducked Luther's blow, locked fingers together, and brought fisted hands up hard under Gibbs's chin. He knocked Luther flat, and yelled: "You men better listen to me! You're damned fools if you think Luther is goin' to share anything with you! He won't . . ."

Roaring fury, the outlaw leader scrambled back to his feet, his pistol in his hand.

Buck shifted his attention from Luther's underlings back to Gibbs. "You won't kill me, Luther. You do, and it'd ruin your darlin' little plan."

"Like hell! I'd just as lief bring you in dead as alive, Fyffe!"

"No, you wouldn't." Buck grinned past bared teeth. "I'm the one who ran you down . . . brought you in for tria . . . testified against you . . . was transportin' you to jail. You kill me, think of all the satisfaction you'll miss if you pull this off and I spend fifteen years in Yuma in your place while you live high on all that money." Feet spread to the extent of the rope between his ankles, and hands still locked and ready, his crouch deepened. "You know that if you do tell these men where you hid the loot, they'll desert you and kill each other to see who can get to the cache first. That money is your only hold over them. They're not your friends, Luther, they're merely coyotes slinkin' round the fringes just waitin' to steal your hard-won evening meal!"

Surprisingly, Blue Paley breathed in his soft Georgia drawl: "You sure have a low opinion of us, you stinkin' Yankee-lovah, you callin' us coyotes and scavengahs and the like. I take pure offense at some abolitionist callin' me names. I don't know 'bout the rest of you boys, but I'm with Luther all the way. What do y'all say?"

Gibbs tensed when he turned from Buck to survey the group. Moses Little nodded agreement, but added: "Still, the marshal's got a point. Luther, how come you ain't tol' us where the cache is hid?"

"When did I have the opportunity to do it? Like I said, we got separated after the holdup. Then Fyffe here got me before I could get back to you. Then there was the trial, and then . . ."

"Well, we're all together now," Ed Fisher put in. "I, for one, would like to hear what happened to our money. I mean, s'pose your horse falls and you git killed, boss? Then nobody would git the benefit of all our hard work and plannin' and the like."

"I'll tell you boys," Luther said, "but not in front of him." He indicated Fyffe with a wave of his pistol.

"Oh, well, that can be taken care of real easy. Men . . ." Moses rose and beckoned the others.

Buck stepped back from Gibbs when he saw the group closing in on him. He sent Little to the dirt with a well-placed two-handed blow, but Fisher and Lambert came up behind him, grabbed his arms, and held on. Blue Paley lunged at him and got a little too close for his own good. When the outlaw stepped across the rope between Fyffe's ankles, Buck used the men holding him as a brace, folded his body, caught Paley's leg with the rope, and the outlaw flipped over backward.

All four—Paley, Fyffe, and the two holding him—went down. Buck tried to roll free, but Cecil lunged in, snagged the chain between their prisoner's wrists, dragged Fyffe's arms out flat on the ground, dropped a knee onto the chain, and jammed hands onto Fyffe's elbows to immobilize him. With Jake Lambert lying across his legs, Clapp restraining his arms, and Fisher and Paley clutching his shirt and hair, Buck could do nothing but breathe hard and glare at Moses Little when the man snarled a wordless sound of fury, wiped at blood running from his mouth, and again lunged.

"Moses, halt!" Luther yelled.

Surprised, Little jerked back. He scowled at Gibbs and began hotly: "But, boss, that sonovabitch . . ."

"No, Moses, you're too riled. Looks to me like you're fixin' to kill him. We want him alive."

"You want him alive! I don't give a shit if he's livin' or dead, and nobody fool-punches me like that and gits away with it!"

Luther said shrewdly: "All right, you'll get your chance, but we'll do it my way. You boys hold that bastard till Moses cools off some, and then we'll let matters proceed." Gibbs spread a sardonic grin all over Buck before he noted: "But that both of us got blue eyes and brown hair and are about the same build, Fyffe, we don't look a lot alike. I figger by the time Moses gets done with you, nobody will notice the difference.

"Moses, you got yourself back together yet? Yes? All right, I want him well messed up but nothin' broke, you understand? So someone seein' him can't rightly tell what he looks like till it's too late and we're long gone. You be careful, now. Do it right, Moses."

"You bet, Luther," Little breathed.

The men holding Fyffe down leaned more heavily on him, and Buck had no choice but to take what came at him.

* * * * *

It was well into the middle of the night before Buck came around. When he got his brain working again, he discovered that his wrists were now manacled behind him and that he lay on his side with his feet pulled up and his bound ankles tethered to his wrists.

He stifled a groan and lifted his head to look around, had to blink several times to clear his sight enough to see the outlaws rolled in their blankets here and there. Near the fire, Blue Paley slept drooped over the rifle across his knees.

Fyffe swallowed the old iron taste of blood that fouled his mouth and let his head fall back to the ground. He hurt so generally that he couldn't pinpoint any particular spot to call most painful—the beating Moses Little had administered had been coldly and efficiently done—but he supposed he should be thankful to still be alive.

He lay resting for a few moments and used the time to listen hard around the camp. A few snores. The heavy, even puffing of sleeping breath. That was all. Trying to make as little noise as possible himself, he reached weak and shaking fingers for the rope between his wrists and ankles, located the nearest knot, and went to work on it.

When the outlaws awoke in the early dawn, their prisoner had vanished.

* * * * *

The off-riders were in a quandary. They had expected the outlaws to immediately kill Fyffe; that they hadn't was a puzzlement to them. Now, though, it might be a stroke of luck. If Buck actually eluded the hardcases, the Gibbs gang might give it up and head back north. But it also meant they themselves had to be extra wary, else in the search for Fyffe, they were discovered.

They watched with careful eyes, and prepared to bolt if Luther and his men got too close.

CHAPTER FOUR

Because his wrists were manacled behind him, Buck couldn't mount a horse without help. He seriously considered trying, but better judgment counseled against it; if he took a flying leap onto an unsaddled animal and fell off the other side, the resulting commotion would surely awaken the outlaws. Considering also that he might break something in the process, he did the next best thing and cat-footed it out into the darkness.

He didn't try to go very far. He reasoned that Luther and crew would expect him to head for the horizon, but like attempting a no-hands mount, dashing around the desert when he couldn't see where he was going wasn't advisable. Even so, he located what might have been the only hiding place within twenty miles by the simple expedient of accidentally falling into it.

It was a hole in the ground where past flash floods had washed out a four-foot-deep crevice beneath a creosote bush's root system at the edge of a dry wash. He came up on the arroyo lip unexpectedly, stepped aside to keep from falling over the edge, his foot met air, and he plunged onto soft sandy soil.

Unhurt, but frozen in expectation of meeting an angry rattler or other nocturnal predator in the narrow confines, he held his breath and waited for an attack that never came. Little by little, he relaxed. Above him, the patch of sky showed dimming stars as night gave way to predawn. All around him in the hole was nothing but the adobe smell of dry dirt and the medicine scent of the few creosote roots his plunge had broken.

Moving cautiously, still half expecting a sidewinder's strike or a scorpion's sting, he squirmed until he gained a little room in the hole. His first order of business was to try to get his hands in front of him. There was only some three inches of chain between the wristbands—he was long-legged and not that flexible in a restricted space—still, he began to work the chain down over his buttocks.

Sky showing through the lacework of exposed roots was pale dawn-blue by the time he had his body painfully folded and his right leg through the circle of his linked arms. He paused to rest, and, with motionlessness, noticed the faint vibration of hoofbeats transmitted through the soil. He grinned sourly; Gibbs and his men were awake, had discovered him gone, and were searching for him. He didn't know what kind of spoor he had left on the desert. In the dark, it had been impossible to see if he made tracks in the dirt, broken twigs and so on, but he'd been more interested in putting some distance between himself and the gang than . . .

A shadow froze him briefly, but then he frowned. Whatever was up there didn't seem to be human. His heart bounced and began a hard beat of alarm. He resumed trying to work the chain from between his thighs down over his left leg. Eyes warily on the rim of earth above him, he had links below his knee when a coyote peered in at him, yipped, and made a tentative snap toward him before it darted back out of sight.

"Shit," he breathed, and slid the chain toward his ankle.

The coyote—or a different one—was back. Buck didn't know if it was the blood dried on his face and shirt or his relative helplessness that drew the varmints, whether they were just playing or intended to attack, but now two heads poked over the rim. The animals whined, yipped, and growled as they made aborted lunges at him. He thought that coyotes normally hunted alone and for nothing larger than rabbits or prairie dogs. He wasn't too up on their habits; maybe they were mates. It seemed late in the year for breeding season, but perhaps the bitch had a growing litter she needed to feed. Or perhaps the coyotes were only having fun; whatever, the two continued to dance at the hole rim, make unfulfilled lunges at him, always leaping out of sight between snaps.

"Get away from me, you mangy varmints!" His shouted whisper drove the animals back only momentarily.

Thankful that he wasn't wearing spurs, Buck yanked the chain over his bootheel. Though it had taken him more than an hour to do it, now he had his hands in front of him. He scraped dirt from the side of the crevice. The next time a coyote head appeared against the sky, he threw the clod in the animal's face. The coyotes shrieked, wheeled, and vanished, and Buck snorted to himself—one show of resistance from him, and the cowardly critters were gone.

He looked at his hands. His wrists were sore and metal edges had pressed red streaks into the base of his thumbs, though nothing bled. The rest of him ached, but all in all, he wasn't too badly injured. His major problems were that he had no food, no water, no weapons, and no transportation, and wherever he was, it was a hell of a long way to civilization of any kind.

All right, what to do? Perhaps his best bet would be to stay right where he was today, lay low, rest, and hope that Luther Gibbs and his bunch would give up the search and go their way.

Yesterday, they had crossed a road he thought was the one leading inland from Ehrenberg on the Colorado River. He would go back to it and turn west toward the town. If a stagecoach or riders came by, maybe they would stop and pick him up, though considering the mess he was at the moment, the chains and all, they might not want to chance it.

If he could make it to Ehrenberg, he would go directly to the sheriff's office, explain the situation, and then he would track Luther. No way was Gibbs going to get away from . . .

Something snapped above him. Scowling, he pressed closer to the shadowed wall beneath the thickest part of the creosote roots, because coyotes didn't crush twigs underfoot. He knew who was up there. He glanced quickly around the hole, searching for a loose rock, a piece of wood, anything to use as a weapon, but found nothing. He almost stopped breathing while he waited. He saw two shadows slip up the far wall when the men approached, and then heads blotted the sky. And two six-guns became pointed at him.

Jake Lambert chortled: "Look what we got here! I wondered what was drawin' varmints, and there ya are, Fyffe!"

"The great Buck Fyffe, betrayed by a couple of flea-bit coyotes," Ed Fisher chuckled. "Ol' Luther is sure gonna get a laugh outta that! You gonna come out of there on your own, or do we gotta dig you out?" Fisher thumbed the hammer on his weapon.

A leaden grimness settled into Buck's gut. He took a deep breath, gritted teeth, and pushed himself upright; there was no sense in fighting, because they had him. Silently maligning coyotes and bad luck, he climbed out of the hole and merely stood waiting, but flinched when Fisher pulled the trigger and the bullet sang past his ear. It was a signal to the other searchers to let them know they had located the quarry.

Off in the distance, three riders wheeled their mounts and headed this way.

"Ed, I'll keep 'im covered till the others git here if you'd kindly go git our horses for us."

"Sure 'nough, Jake . . . but watch him. He's one sneaky bastard."

"He tries anything now, I'll just plug 'im in the laig. That oughtta slow 'im down some."

"Hell, why don't ya do it anyway? Leastwise, then we won't have to worry about him pullin' somethin' like this ag'in."

"Good idea." Lambert aimed at Buck's thigh.

"Hold it!" Chain clattered when Fyffe flung up his arms. "You don't have to do that. I know when I've had it. I made my bid and lost the hand . . . I'm folded, all right? You've already shot me once. You've beat up on me, locked me in handcuffs, and have run me down. Let's leave it at that, all right?"

"'Side," said Ed Fisher, grinning from where he led two saddled horses toward them, "Luther might take offense. Too many holes in his prize catch could be hard to explain down in Yuma." He dropped reins, picked a lariat from where it was tied with saddle strings, and nodded to Lambert. "Keep 'im covered, Jake." Watching Buck warily, he stepped forward and snapped: "Let's have them arms down, Fyffe." He tied the end of the rope securely to the chain.

Lambert kept a bead on Buck until Fisher had mounted, then leathered his sidearm, swung astride his own mount, and the two led off at a brisk trot. Fyffe was forced to nearly run to keep from being jerked off his feet and dragged. The other searchers joined them. Whooping and laughing, and flicking

the ends of reins at him, they herded Buck across the desert
floor and back into the campsite.

* * * * *

"Damn!" one of the off-riders breathed to another, and handed
over the glasses. "They got 'im back. Well, hell, I guess this means
we go on clean to Yuma, don't it."

"Shit, yore right," the second snarled. "Oh, wel . . ."

Together, they moved to where the third held the horses
out of sight, and mounted up.

* * * * *

Grinning broadly, Gibbs rose when the group arrived. Freshly
shaven and with coffee cup in hand, he sauntered to where Buck
dripped sweat and panted desperately. "Good try, Babyface, I
have to admit." He looked Fyffe up and down. "I wouldn't have
thought you could get out of here last night, but you did it,
din't you. Where'd you find him, boys?"

Chuckling, Jake explained about the coyotes.

Luther shook his head. "Coyotes, you say! Tsk! Who'd have
thought it. Moses, give our guest some water. He looks like he
needs it. And, Babyface, I even saved you some breakfast over
there. Set and eat, then we'll be on our way."

Buck caught the canteen Little tossed to him, lifted it with
both hands, and began to drink. He wasn't prepared for the fist
Gibbs abruptly rammed into his belly. Water sprayed from his
open mouth when he went down, choking and on his knees at
the outlaw leader's feet. He barely heard Luther snarl: "That's
for the trouble you put us to this mornin', Fyffe. Break camp,
boys. We got a ways to go today." Gibbs picked the canteen out

of the dirt before it emptied, and capped it. "And Cecil, tomor-row mornin', I want you to shave."

Clapp ran fingers over chin stubble below his thick black mustache. "Why the hell for, boss? I ain't seein' no woman tomorrow."

"No, you're not. But when you dress like a banker and act like a banker, you can go into a bank without them expectin' you to hold the place up. You dress like a lawman and look like a lawman, you can pass for one." He flourished a hand at Buck back on his feet but swaying unsteadily under heavy morning sunlight. "Does that look like a federal marshal, I ask you? Not hardly! You're s'posed to be my deputy. When we hit Yuma, I want you to look the part."

"Gotcha." Cecil grinned. "You want Fyffe to eat?"

"Hell, I don't care if he eats or not. He'd have stuck around, we would have fed and watered him. Maybe a little less consid-eration on our part will make him think twice before he tries somethin' again.

"Put him on his horse and lock him down. Coyotes, eh? Would you have thought it! Ha!"

The day wore on in heat and pain. Buck didn't make another escape attempt. He merely sat his horse, head bowed beneath sun glare, and tried to last.

At noon, the outlaws halted briefly. Gibbs gave Fyffe food and some water, and after that, Buck felt a little better. He tried to wash his face with water poured into his palm, but Luther slapped his hand away. The outlaws wanted their prisoner to look the part. Buck knew he did look the part, but let it go. There was always tomorrow.

They posted two guards that night to preclude a repeat of Fyffe's escape into the darkness. It was wasted effort; Buck merely lay in the dirt, his hands once again locked behind him, ankles securely bound but not tied to his wrists this time, and slept like the dead. He was considerably refreshed the next morning, felt a lot better until—shortly after noon and off in the distance—he saw the town of Yuma crouched at the feet of the adobe growth sprouting atop Prison Hill.

* * * * *

The off-riders continued to follow, but staying out of sight grew progressively more difficult as vegetation thinned and the landscape became ever more barren and forbidding. Still, with extreme care, they managed, because they were accomplished predators.

CHAPTER FIVE

"Now." Luther halted his horse and became serious. "Jake, Blue, Ed, and Moses, you boys split off here, go on into town, find yourselves a nice cool saloon, have a drink or two, and wait. I and Steve . . ." He nodded significantly at Cecil Clapp. ". . . will deliver Mistuh Gibbs here to his permanent residence, then we'll meet you there. Then, after all the shoutin' dies down . . . after you've had a few shots of good whiskey and maybe a whore or two . . . we'll leave town in ones and twos, join up out here, and go get our take. Start really enjoyin' life."

He slid a look at Buck watching and listening silently. "And, Babyface, before you ask, I did tell my men where I hid the loot. And see . . . they're still with me. That's loyalty, right? We're friends! Partners! Whaddya got to say now?"

"My compliments," Fyffe murmured dryly, and left it at that. He looked back toward the prison. From this distance, and shielded behind heat waves shimmering above the sand, he couldn't make out details, but the place looked ominous. It brought a sick, muddy-cold fear to his belly. He worked hard to subdue it, because he needed a clear head now as never before.

The outlaw quartet whooped, saluted Gibbs, and spurred their mounts toward Yuma. Luther and Cecil held steady until the others had put a goodly distance between them. Then Gibbs nodded to Fyffe. "Come on, Babyface, let's get this finished up so Steve and me can wet our whistles in town along with friends." He jerked the lead rope to Buck's horse, led off at a fast walk, and shouted more than sang:

> "I came to Ala-bama with my ban-jo on my
> knee . . .
> I'm goin' to Loo-si-anna, my true love for
> to see!
> It rained all night the day I left, the weather
> it was dry . . ."

"Luther, don't you know any other song?" Buck scowled.

Gibbs curled a sneer at him, but shut up and urged his mount into a canter.

* * * * *

Two of the off-riders also broke off and followed the major portion of the Gibbs gang into town. The third tagged after Luther, Cecil, and their prisoner. Why, he wondered, was Gibbs actually headed for the prison?

* * * * *

As they approached from out of the northeast, Buckley Fyffe got a better view of the prison. It was situated on a solid stone bluff above Yuma. Beyond a point of land to the south, the Gila River met the Colorado, and beyond that, lay the Gila River Valley.

Farther southwest in the Sonoran desert, as hot, barren, and dangerous as Fyffe had ever seen a land be, was Pilot Knob, where Arizona, California, and Mexico met. What with the two rivers, the open and mostly barren land, and the way the guard towers were set, it seemed to him the likelihood of a successful escape from Yuma Prison would be all but impossible.

As they neared, he saw that the prison was still under construction, being cut into and built atop the granite schist and chalk mesa. He looked again at the Colorado. On the California side of where the river coursed swiftly through a narrowing of banks stood Fort Yuma. There appeared to be only a few hundred feet between the banks in one spot, but eddies and disturbed surface water betrayed vicious currents below; he doubted anyone could swim it and escape that way. The authorities had chosen their site well.

He returned his examination to the unfinished prison as Gibbs led up the steep road winding from the desert floor to the top of the hill. Part of the place was fenced by a wooden stockade, but a thick stone and adobe wall was in progress, being constructed by men in vertically-striped uniforms while vigilant guards on the ground and patrolling the finished wall top watched.

One of those guards, his .44-40 Winchester rifle cradled in his arms, his expression stern and suspicious around a bushing brown mustache, challenged their arrival.

Luther was prepared. He had Buck's identification wallet ready in hand and flourished it as he reined in. "US Federal Marshal Buckley Fyffe bringin' Luther Gibbs in from Prescott under Yavapai Judge Hauser's orders. That there is my deputy, Steve Larson. You should be expectin' us."

The guard looked over at Buck sitting grimly astride his mount, his wrists chained to the saddle, his bloodstained shirt filthy, three-days' growth of beard and lingering bruises marring his face, and nodded. He jabbed a finger toward where a low, square building sporting a deep-roofed porch sat outside the walls and to the right of the huge, arched, strap-iron main gate. Beside the one-story building rose a larger one girdled by a second-floor balcony.

He said: "First house is the office, Marshal. That next to it is the guards' quarters. I don't know if the superintendent is there presently, but the turnkey is, and he's the one you want to see anyway. His name's Godfrey McHugh, and he'll do the honors. Uh . . . looks like you had some trouble gettin' your man here."

Luther grinned, nodded, and, the wallet still in hand, beckoned to Clapp, who scowled at convicts laboring in the broiling sun. Cecil seemed as tense as a coiled rattler.

Even in the heat, Buck felt the rise of a kind of icy shuddering desperation as he continued to scrutinize the area. He noted the guards, their sidearms and shoulder guns, their watchfulness. He saw prisoners—one dragging a lead ball by a heavy two-foot-long chain attached to his right ankle—less than enthusiastic at their labor, and decided he could do nothing out here. If he tried to escape Gibbs and Clapp now, prison guards would join in and he would probably be shot down without ado. He had to wait until he could talk to the superintendent or assistant superintendent. Maybe then . . .

Gibbs and Clapp led Fyffe's horse with them when they headed toward the prison office. Clapp kept a close eye on their captive while Luther dismounted, ground-tethered his horse, and strode purposefully into the building's interior.

Buck slid a grim sidelong look at Cecil when Clapp grinned and murmured softly: "This is it, boy. How you like the look of your new home, eh?" When Fyffe didn't respond, Cecil snorted: "Haw!" Nothing more was said because Luther reappeared at the door together with a round-faced, walrus-mustached man dressed in a navy blue, brass-buttoned uniform complete with a kepi-style gold-braid-decorated cap that, except for the heavy weapon on his hip, made him look like a train conductor.

"That's him, Mistuh McHugh." Gibbs nodded toward Buck.

The assistant superintendent held the incarceration order Gibbs had given him. He said briskly: "All right, gentlemen, bring him in, and I'll fill out the paperwork." He raised his voice. "Mr. Parrish!"

One of the guards lifted his head from where he looked off across the valley, and turned toward the office.

McHugh continued: "Mr. Parrish, will you provide a little security here, please?" Paper in one hand and the other palm on his gun butt, McHugh watched while Clapp dismounted, pulled the key from his pants pocket, unlocked Fyffe from the saddle, and dragged him off the horse. The guard walked up and took a wide-footed stance between them and the trail to the desert. None of them noticed the man on the dark roan mare talking to a different guard across the yard.

Under Gibbs's and McHugh's careful eyes, Clapp shoved Buck into the office. The room was square, sparsely furnished, and though all doors and windows were open to catch any passing breeze, only slightly cooler than the yard.

Clapp halted Fyffe in front of a table on which a thick book lay open beside a penholder and inkwell. McHugh seated himself in the chair on the other side of the table, turned an oversized page, and dipped the pen, and Buck saw that the book contained printed forms to be filled out as required. He was about to go down in Yuma Territorial Prison history.

McHugh consulted the incarceration order, muttered, "Luther Ben Gibbs," and began to write on the top line.

"No, sir!" Fyffe said abruptly. "I'm not Gibbs!" When

McHugh looked up at him, Buck tilted his head toward Luther and continued rapidly, "My name is Buckley Fyffe. That man is Luther Gibbs, and the one who calls himself Steve Larson is . . ."

Clapp scowled and made a grab for Buck, but Luther flung an arm across Cecil's chest to stop him and said mildly: "No, no, Steve, let it go. I want to hear what he's got to say."

Almost breathlessly, Buck explained to the turnkey everything that had happened on the trail between here and Prescott. While Clapp glowered, Luther merely stood by, arms folded now, a slight smile on his lips and humor dancing in his blue eyes.

Buck finished: ". . . and if you let them walk out of here, sir, you'll have just lost Gibbs and one of his men."

Luther nodded. He asked: "You done, Gibbs? You got that all out of your system now? Yeah?" He sighed heavily. "Mistuh McHugh, we had one helluva time on our way with ol' Luther, here. He tried to escape at every opportunity. Wel . . ."He flourished a hand at Buck. "As you can see, sir, we had to physically restrain him, had to run him down . . . even had to shoot him once to stop him. Hell," he laughed shortly, "hadn't been for a couple of curious coyotes, we would have lost him. As you can see, he's a real unruly prisoner. I suggest you take immediate steps to . . . uh . . . subdue him, else you gonna have one prime troublemaker in your midst."

"Sir," Fyffe thrust chained hands toward McHugh, "sir, you've got to believe me! I'm not Luther Gibbs!"

Abruptly, Gibbs lost his laugh. He grabbed his pistol from its holster and jammed it against Fyffe's ear, and snarled: "Shut up, Gibbs, I've had enough of you! I and Steve want to get this done with and get on our way, so answer Mistuh McHugh's questions and nothin' else!"

A feeling of outraged futility made Buck whirl on Gibbs. He gritted hotly: "You're not goin' to get away with this, Luther!

I never lost a man yet, and you're not gonna be my first! You'll never get to spend Southwestern's money, Luther, because I'll get out of here and run you down, and you can count on that!"

"Well, I guess you got a potential escapee here, don'tcha, Mistuh McHugh?" Luther slid the sidearm back into leather. "Uh . . . if we could get on with this . . ."

Hard-eyed, the turnkey nodded. He dipped the pen again, finished filling in the name space, then wrote behind "SENTENCE: 15 YEARS FROM JUNE 30, 1877, #109." In the space labeled: "NO. OF COMMITMENT," he wrote: "*One*." He continued to fill in spaces until he came to "RACE," then looked up at Buck. "You're white? Any Indian or Mexican blood? Any Negrah?"

"No," Fyffe snarled.

"Nativity?"

"Virginia."

"Religion?"

"Christian."

"Hat size?"

Buck laughed in disbelief. "Why d'you care?"

"We will issue you a hat here, Mr. Gibbs."

Fyffe swallowed. He looked briefly at Luther smirking beside him and fought down a surge of rage, choked out: "S-Six and seven-eighths."

McHugh noted that the incoming prisoner's forehead was intelligent, that his hair was light brown, and his eyes blue, then asked him his shoe size.

"Ten."

McHugh had heard that Gibbs was thirty-five, stood five, eleven tall, weighed one hundred eighty-five pounds, noted that his carriage was erect, and so on. He said to Luther: "I'll fill the rest of this out after he has had a bath and has been shaved face and head, Marshal. I'll give you your receipt . . . then you can go about your business. No need for you and your deputy to wait around."

"I appreciate your consideration, Mistuh McHugh. I don't know about Steve, here, but after what we been through gettin' Gibbs here, I'm 'bout to perish for a glass of good whiskey."

McHugh smiled, his lips tight beneath his mustache. He reached for a different book and wrote on a perforated slip:

#109. Yuma, Arizona, June 30, 1877. Received of Buckley Fyffe United States Federal Marshal Luther Ben Gibbs, convicted in the 3rd Judicial District of the crime of Grand Larceny in the First Degree and sentenced to be imprisoned in the Territorial Penitentiary at Yuma for the term of Fifteen Years.

He signed it: "*Godfrey L. McHugh, Asst. Superintendent.*" He tore the slip at the perforations and handed the receipt to Gibbs.

As Luther tucked the paper into the leather wallet, Buck tried one more time. He said urgently: "Mr. McHugh, you're lettin' Luther Gibbs and Cecil Clapp walk out of here scot-free! Mr. McHugh, you have to listen to me, Mr. McHugh . . . I am Buckley Fyffe, not him, and if . . ."

"Parrish!" McHugh called. When the guard who had been standing outside the door looked into the room, the turnkey rose and continued: "Get one of the other men to help you, and after Marshal Fyffe removes the handcuffs, bring the prisoner." He turned back to Luther. "A pleasure working with you, Marshal. I hope you and Deputy Larson have a safe ride home."

Luther was unlocking Buck's wrists. Expression mocking, he met Fyffe's eyes, flexed brows once, and asserted: "Oh, the pleasure is all mine, Mistuh McHugh. No doubt about that."

With two armed guards barring the office door and no

one listening to him, Buck watched helplessly while Gibbs and Clapp took their leave, mounted up outside, and reined their horses toward the trail leading down from Prison Hill. The two outlaws didn't notice the man kick his dark roan mare into motion from where he had been watching convicts laboring to build adobe mud bricks at the east yard outside the stockade and partially raised wall. The man followed at a discreet distance when the two headed toward the tiny town of Yuma. He turned his head to look back at the prison briefly, muttered, "Sorry, Marsha . . . but them's the breaks sometimes," and nudged his horse onward.

In the office, McHugh said sternly to Buck: "You will be processed now, Mr. Gibbs. We like to think we run this institution as humanely as possible under the circumstances, but since you appear to be seriously recalcitrant, I feel you must learn the error of your ways immediately to forestall future, more unpleasant remedies. Men, after he is prepared, give him twenty-four hours in the Dark Room."

Buck was hustled through the sale puerta, the main gate commonly called the "sally port." He was stripped, ordered to bathe, and dressed in vertical gray-and-black stripes and heavy boots. His face was shaved by the prison barber; then, he sat watching his hair fall onto his thighs when the man clipped it short before also shaving his skull. A round tag bearing the number 109 was affixed to his chest, and he was backed into a corner beside a wall mirror that—when his picture was taken—showed his full face and, in the mirror, his profile.

McHugh accompanied him and the guards through each operation, occasionally making notes on a small pad so he could later complete "Gibbs's" prison record. The notes included the comment: "Gunshot wound, shallow graze, lower rib cage, left side."

Buck was then taken to a hole in the hill at the rear of the prison area where two metal doors stood open at either end of a tunnel some six feet long. Beyond lay a lightless room about fifteen feet across. It was centered by a heavy eight-by-ten by five-feet-high strap-iron cage.

Another guard trotted up carrying a full canteen. Fyffe automatically grabbed the bottle when the man shoved it at him. Once again, he yelled to McHugh: "Dammit, man, you're letting Gibbs get away!"

The guards, one on either side of him, seized his arms, dragged him down the corridor, and shoved him into the cage. He shouted over the clang of the closing gate: "I tell you, I'm Buckley Fyffe! United States Marshal Buck Fyffe, and you . . .!"

The guards turned, left, slammed and locked the tunnel's metal doors after them, and then Buck was alone in stifling, totally silent, absolute darkness.

CHAPTER SIX

The canteen clutched to his chest with his right arm so he wouldn't lose it in the darkness, the fingers of his left drifting over the iron-strap grill, and head and shoulders bent beneath the low ceiling, Buck walked around and around the inner perimeter of the cage. There wasn't far to go. The room may have been relatively large, but the cage wasn't. Still, he walked, because if he stopped, he knew that rage, frustration, and maybe even fear would overcome him and he might end up bashing his brains out against metal he couldn't penetrate.

When he began to see ghosts floating in the air around him, pale green-gold shapes he knew weren't really there, he figured it was his eyes trying to see something and shut them. That helped some, but not much.

He kept walking. His footsteps on the grating beneath him and his breathing were the only sounds in the cell until he said softly: "For the first time, I'm glad you're dead, Laurie . . . you and little Phoebe. Better for you to be dead than to have me just vanish on you . . . like Steve has vanished on Rosie . . . never to know what happened . . . for years, havin' to wait and wonder whether you are a wife or a widow . . ."

His voice drifted away. He kept walking. After a while, he said more firmly: "But I'll get out of here, Laurie, that's a fact. You wait and see if I don't. I don't know how yet, but I will, you can count on that, Laurie. And then, I'm after Luther Gibbs . . . you can count on that, too, Laurie."

He kept walking. Around and around.

"It rained all night the day I left, the weather, it was dry. The sun so hot, I froze to death, Susanna, don't you . . . Damn you, Luther, now you got me doin' it!"

He stopped walking and slid down metal to sit on the grill, uncapped the canteen, and gulped at it but nearly spit the water out at the first mouthful. It was so muddy-thick that he wondered briefly whether it was part of his punishment or if that was the way all water tasted here. He lowered the container for a moment and ground grit between his teeth before he took another swallow, be damned the consistency. Again holding the capped canteen close, this time in both arms, he lay over onto his side, drew up his knees, and hoped his eyes were closed.

A clang and a blast of light awoke Buck. He shoved himself up to sit and blinked to get his eyes working again. A guard entered, thrust a loaf of bread through the hole between the horizontal and vertical cage lattice, dropped it, then left without saying a word.

When the double doors slammed shut, darkness seemed twice as dense to Buck. Swearing under his breath, the canteen still in his left hand, and on his knees, he felt around for the bread. He finally located it, knee-walked back to the cage edge, sat, braced his back against the crosshatch, and ate. Drank mud again. Leaned his naked skull against iron and stared into nothingness.

"If I was Luther Gibbs, what would I do now that I've got myself free and clear of the law?" Shortly, he murmured: "And if I was Buckley Fyffe stuck in Yuma Prison, how would I get out?"

He pondered those two questions for what may have been only moments or may have been half a century—there was no time in the Dark Room. Bread and a fresh canteen came on one more occasion; then, much later, the doors crashed open, and two guards entered.

They unlocked the gate and beckoned. One snapped: "Time's up, Gibbs. Come on out of there. Time to get to work."

Buck decided that he was well-rested, if not amply fed, and that he would handle each occasion as it arose. He nodded, stepped out of the cage, handed the canteen to one of the guards, and said: "There's about two inches of silt in the bottom of that, sir."

"You better get used to it, Gibbs. We got a real water problem here. Even the townsfolk have to settle the mud in water barrels. Move it."

Buck moved. If it was twenty-four hours since his incarceration, it must be shortly after noon; the heavy sun staggered him back into the tunnel briefly until a guard's palm between his shoulder blades forced him out into the glare.

Shading his eyes with an arm and blinking behind abrupt tears brought on by the light, he looked around. Everything appeared to be exactly the same as yesterday; hot sun, beige dust, beige buildings, lackadaisical work crews laboring beneath well-armed guards' narrow stares.

Instead of being immediately put to work, Fyffe was taken by the guards to a side building and given a hat, another pair of underdrawers, another pair of pants, two handkerchiefs, some socks, and two towels. They also provided him with a toothpick, toothbrush, and two combs (though considering his lack of hair, these seemed redundant), one coarse and one a fine-tooth louse rake. His two sheets and pillowcases were marked "#109" with India ink.

Carrying his gear, he was escorted to his cell. It was nothing more than a dome-ceilinged eight-by-nine-foot hole hollowed out of the stone hill and fitted with an iron-grill door. Inside were two triple-decker wooden bunk-racks, a bucket honey pot—and vermin. Buck noted cockroaches thick on the walls, and when he put his supplies on what appeared to be an unoccupied bunk, he disturbed scores of tiny flat brown wingless insects from between joints in the frame. They scurried in the light only momentarily before they hurried back into hiding.

Day one gone, he thought grimly. *Home, sweet home. Where are Luther and his men now?*

* * * * *

Yesterday, the man on the roan mare had joined his two companions as they kept an eye on the major portion of the Gibbs gang. The three of them went to the saloon called the Arizona Club for a drink and to continue their surveillance, but shook their heads in stunned wonder at what happened shortly thereafter. In fact, it damned near boggled their minds.

* * * * *

Buck's cellmates were Burt Loftus, John Burnside, Jim Pye, and two Mexican nationals, Ygnacio Santos and Domingo Gomez, in for selling liquor and guns to the Indians, robbery, robbery, assault, and grand larceny, respectively. Loftus was even smaller, more swarthy, and beadier-eyed than either Santos or Gomez. Burnside, for all that he was in for robbery, was tall, slim, blond, and assumed the languid air of English aristocracy. Pye was short, thin, and had he had hair, red-headed. All five eyed Buck when they were herded into the cell to rest a while before queuing up in the dinner chow line.

Fyffe was lying on the top left-hand bunk, but sat up when the men arrived. Careful not to hit his naked skull on the stone ceiling low above him, he swung his feet over the edge of the inch-thick, straw-padded mattress, braced palms on the wooden frame, and nodded warily to them—he didn't know whether he had friends or foes here.

He had pondered what he would say when asked his name. He wasn't going to answer to Luther Gibbs if he could help it, though circumstances might arise when he had to do it merely to stay out of the Dark Room and to survive. It might even be more dangerous to admit to being Buckley Fyffe in case one or more of the inmates knew the name belonged to a US marshal and took an opportunity for some kind of revenge. When Loftus eyed him coolly and asked, "Who the hell are you?" Fyffe thought of the name Gibbs called him.

"BF," he answered.

"BF what?"

Buck shrugged. "Nothin'. Just BF."

"Ha! Yore mama wasn't much on imagination, was she!"

Buck let that go.

"Whatchoo in fer?" Santos braced a palm on the end of Fyffe's bunk.

Buck looked at the five hardcases eyeing him, at the stone walls and crosshatch strap-iron gate behind them, and felt surrounded. He answered tersely: "Grand larceny."

"Ah!" John Burnside murmured. "You're the one they hustled straight off to the Snake Den!" When Buck scowled at the blond, John explained: "The Dark Room. But I thought your name was . . . uh . . . Gibbs or Gibson or somethin' like that."

"Call me whatever you want," Fyffe snapped. Outside, a triangle clanged. It was dinnertime, and whatever was served, he would at last get to eat. His cellmates didn't seem to be too threatening—so far. Maybe he could actually survive this.

He counted thirty-eight men, including himself, waiting in pairs in line to be fed. He asked Loftus, beside him: "Where are the rest? Don't they get to eat?"

"What rest?" Loftus scowled. "This is all they is right now . . . ain't it 'nough fer ya?"

"But my number is one-oh-nine. I expected to see a lot more inmates."

Loftus showed gaps where teeth were missing when he laughed. "Aw, they started with number one at the outset and jus' kept numberin'. A hunnert and eight men come and went afore you, that's all."

Supper consisted of onion stew, bread, and tea. It wasn't a lot, but it was enough to get Buck through the night. He slept relatively comfortably, except to scratch when bedbugs bit at him, and once to fend Burnside off when the man made immoral advances to him. He convinced the robber he wasn't interested in that sort of thing. Since his first, "Get away from me," hadn't seemed strong enough, his second, "No!" followed by a reinforcing fist in John's teeth brought an end to it.

Breakfast the next morning was beef and boiled potatoes, both leaving an odd, musty, almost burning aftertaste on the back of his tongue. That was accompanied by more bread, and coffee that barely overrode the muddy taint of the water that brewed it. But he felt all right as he again stood in line with the others, this time to receive today's work assignment.

He and eleven other inmates were sent to the rear of the

prison to break large rocks into gravel, and then the gravel into sand. One of the laborers was prisoner Number 36, who dragged the thirty-pound ball and chain behind him, and when Buck got a closer look at the man, his heart bounced.

Pete Roy. Wouldn't you know it! Pete Roy, who he had run down and hauled in for robbing the US Mail. Now, the problem was: if he knew Roy, would the man also recognize him?

In fact, Pete eyed him on the way to the rock pile, frowned, and said: "You look familiar to me, hombre. Do I know you? What's yer name?"

Buck ran a hand over his face and skull—the top of his head felt like the mohair upholstery on a sofa cushion as hair became stubble—and growled: "Luther Gibbs . . . and I never seen ya."

Roy cast him a curious, unsatisfied look. Buck hurried on ahead to separate himself from the man; unhindered by a ball and chain, he could move faster than Pete. He seized one of the sledgehammers and attacked the stone pile, kept his head down, and merely worked. Still, he could feel Roy's occasional puzzled scrutiny throughout the day. He discovered, also, that working in the 105- to 110-degree heat, and without hair to sop it up, sweat was a constant problem, burning his eyes and dripping off his nose and chin as though he stood under a hot rain.

Prisoners broke rock every other day. The next day, Buck was assigned to help build the wall. He noted with grim admiration that the relatively soft adobe bricks were stacked and mortared on either side of a heavy iron grating that kept prisoners from cutting through the wall and escaping. The bricks were then faced with a plaster of mud for protection against rain and whitewashed to give the place a finished look.

So far, he got along well with the other prisoners. Burnside didn't approach him again. His third evening in prison, only he, Pye, Burnside, and the two Mexicans occupied their cell, because Burt Loftus had drawn eight hours in the Snake Den for throwing a rock at another inmate. Except for the ever-present cockroaches, bedbugs, and thick water, the food wasn't too bad, even with that strange, acrid aftertaste. His bunk was adequate, the guards didn't seem to be overly brutal, he received a tobacco ration and sat on the sand outside the cell, his back braced against the hot wall, sharing a cheroot with Santos while they watched two others playing checkers by the light of an oil lamp, and he decided that Yuma Territorial Prison wasn't living up to its fledgling reputation.

All that changed midafternoon of his fourth day. Buck was again breaking rocks at the south wall. He stopped work for a moment, leaned the sledgehammer handle against his thigh, and lay his hat on a boulder. As he pulled off his shirt and wadded the garment to use it as a towel to mop at sweat—not that the effort lasted—he noted Pete Roy still dragging the ball and chain and eyeing him as he worked at the next rock pile over. He could almost see wheels turning in Roy's brain, and thought with certainty that one of these damned days, maybe after his hair grew out some, Pete was going to realize who he was. Then, he might be in deep trouble, because Roy was a formidable man, heavy through the chest and shoulders and with thighs like tree trunks.

He nodded to Roy before he flapped his damp shirt, tied the sleeves around his neck, and let the rest hang down his spine like a cape so the body of the garment would shade his back and keep him from getting sunburned. He was reaching for the hat when a howl of fury and running feet behind him barely warned him that the trouble he expected had arrived. Amazingly, it wasn't from Pete.

CHAPTER SEVEN

"There you are, Fyffe, you sonovabitch!" Even red with rage, Moses Little's freshly-shaven face and skull lent him a stark, pale appearance when he lunged at Buck.

Fyffe grabbed the sledgehammer handle and hefted the tool like a weapon. He wondered what the hell Moses was doing here. He thought Gibbs and his gang would have been long gone to retrieve and enjoy the fruits of their robbery!

Little, now #110, ignored both the sledgehammer Buck held and the guards who scowled, shouted after him, and broke into a run toward him. Moses bolted across the open yard, arms spread and hands clutching, and made a dive for Buck. Fyffe sidestepped. The other inmates backed off, frowning and wary, when Little missed seizing Fyffe and fell onto the rock pile. Instantly, Moses scrambled up, whirled to face Buck, and again started for his target, but the guards had arrived. Together, three of them leaped on Little and held him struggling and shouting curses.

Livid with outrage, Moses almost shrieked at Buck who crouched a few feet away with the hammer still in his hands.

"You'd have kept yer mouth shut, Fyffe, it wouldn't have happened, but, no . . . you had to give Luther the idea, din't you, and now they're dead! They're all dead but me and Luther! Even ol' Cecil's dead, and now . . ."

His hand on his sidearm, the turnkey, McHugh, hurried toward them. He asked sternly: "What's going on here?"

One of the guards began: "Gibbs was just breakin' rocks when this new . . ."

"That ain't Luther Gibbs!" Moses yelled, still fighting to get at his target. "That's Marshal Buck Fyffe! Ol' Luther double-crossed us and is now headin' for the cache, and if he hadn't give Gibbs the idea, none of it would have happened! He . . ."

"That's who you are!" Behind the guards, Pete Roy dropped his sledgehammer and, in the same motion, picked up the chain attached to his ankle. The thirty-pound lead ball swinging from his hands, he stepped around the group and toward Buck. Eyes cold and hating above the half smile on his mouth, he growled: "I knew I knew you from some place, you bastard. Marshal Buckley Fyffe, ain't it! By gawd, it is you, you . . ."

Buck's fingers tightened on the hammer handle. He stood his ground but said softly: "I wondered how long it was gonna be before you recognized me, Pete. Keep your distance. From the looks of that ball and chain, you're in enough trouble as it is."

Roy nodded and stopped, but lifted his voice to the other inmates who had ceased work to watch and listen. "Look who we got here, boys! A US marsha . . . one of us, now, ain't he! What one of yore precious laws did you break to have yore own kind turn on you, eh, Marshal? You think you gonna git to be one of us, Marshal? Huh-uh! How long you think you can live before somebody slides a knife into you, eh? You gonna be able to sleep nights now with everybody here knowin' US Federal Marshal Buck Fyffe is . . ."

"You're not Luther Gibbs?" McHugh scowled at Buck.

Fyffe kept his eyes on Roy. All the fight had gone out of Moses; held by the guards, he had stopped struggling and stood with tears of helpless rage streaming down his face, but Pete still swung the ball back and forth on the end of the chain. Given half a chance, Fyffe knew the man would use it on him.

He said to the turnkey: "I told you who I was when Gibbs and Clapp brought me in, Mr. McHugh, but Luther bamboozled you into believing I was him. I don't blame you, sir. Gibbs had it real well set up, but . . ." He looked back at Little. "Moses, what the hell happened?"

"I want to hear the rest of this myself, and so will the superintendent," McHugh said. He motioned to the guards. "Men, bring Gibbs . . . Fyffe . . . whoever he is . . . and Moses Little to the office. You, Roy, put that ball down, and get back to work, or . . ." He let the sentence hang, the threat clear enough.

Reluctantly, Pete stepped back out of the way to let Buck and the guards pass. Fyffe offered the sledgehammer to Roy and met his eyes, murmured: "I may see you later, Pete."

The ball hit the dirt with a heavy thud. Roy grabbed the tool. He snarled: "You bet, Fyffe. I been in the Snake Den so many times, it don't bother me anymore. Next time, I'm gonna earn my stay." He watched Buck, McHugh, the guards, and the heavily gasping Moses Little move on out through the sally port and toward the prison office just beyond.

On the way, Fyffe untied his shirtsleeves from around his neck, slid into the garment, and wiped his face with an arm before he studied Little with narrow eyes. Something strange had happened to the Gibbs gang . . . something he had suggested to Luther? He searched his memory but couldn't come up with a thing.

He wondered if McHugh and the superintendent became

convinced he was who he was, would they let him go or would he have to wait here for some kind of official word to effect his release days or weeks on? If the latter was the case, he would then have to try to live among inmates who knew who he was, because he had no doubts that Pete Roy was spreading the word. He didn't hope for anything, but merely waited, watched, and listened when the group entered the office and a compact, bearded, hazel-eyed man, dressed in a natty business suit rather than a uniform, frowned up from the desk at the left wall of the room.

The superintendent looked to McHugh. "What's going on here, Godfrey?"

"That's what we're trying to find out, sir." The turnkey motioned to Moses. "Would you explain all this, Mr. Little?"

Moses straightened in the guards' grip. Expression drawn, but eyes now dry, he glanced at Buck and said nothing.

Fyffe asked: "What kind of an idea did I give Gibbs, Moses? What was it I said that . . .?"

His words were cut off when Little blurted in what appeared to be a totally wounded outrage: "Out on the trail, you tol' us that once ol' Luther convinced ever'body here he was you, then he'd get the Yuma sheriff to take out the rest of us, and then he'd be a oner with the cash, and that's exactly what he done, you sonovabitch! You'd kept your mouth shut, he'd never have thought of it, and we'd all be rich men, but no . . . now, Jake, Cecil, and Blue are dead . . . Ed Fisher's so shot up, he's never gonna be the same if he ain't dead, too . . ."

Now, Buck recalled the incident. "How? When? It has only been four or five days since . . ."

"Luther and Cecil met us at the Ar'zona Club saloon, like they was supposed to," Moses howled, eyes once again teary. "We set aroun' drinkin' for a while, then Luther digs in his pocket and hands ol' Cecil some of yore money and says . . . 'Steve, go over to the hotel and git us some rooms. We'll stay overnight, play a li'l blackjack, have us a whore or two or three, and lite out tomorrow mornin' fresh-like. Ol' Cecil, he grins and nods and leaves, but he comes back with the Yuma sheriff and 'bout ten deputies, and they don' say nothin', 'cept Cecil, he points us out and says . . . 'There they are!'

"Then, Luther, he leaps up, points his hogleg at us, and says . . . 'Don't move, boys . . . You're all under arrest for robbin' Southwestern of twenty-five thousand dollars.'

"I mean, we all set with our mouths open for a minute before Jake, he yells . . . 'You double-crossin' bastard, you ain't gonna git away with it!' And he goes for his gun, and that starts it.

"The Yuma sheriff and his men take out Jake and Blue and shoot Ed. Me, I hit the floor, and then Luther, he shoots Cecil! I seen 'im! Shot ol' Cec like it was one of us who done it! Kilt him just like that! And when it was all over, they was nobody of us left alive but me and Luther, and the Yuma sheriff says to Luther . . . 'Well, that takes care of the Gibbs gang, 'cept for this one, don't it, Marshal Fyffe?' Luther, he looks at me and says . . . 'Yup, and this one's goin' to jail.'

"I'm tryin' to tell the sheriff that Luther is Luther, but ol' Luther, he looks like he's real put upon, and he pulls out yore papers and shows 'em to the sheriff, and the sheriff and his men believe he's you. They take the boys and Cecil to Boot Hill, Ed off to the doc, and me to jail!"

"So, Luther did the same thing to you he did to me, eh, Moses?" Buck scowled. "I guess he figured if it worked once, it would work twice. But how'd you end up here so fast?"

McHugh, the assistant superintendent, and the guards had been listening silently and somewhat incredulously to all this, but now the superintendent said: "Yuma is the county seat. The judge resides at the courthouse, and . . ."

"Yeah!" Little wailed. "They kep' me in the city jail overnight and the next day, then yeste'day, Luther and the sheriff took me to see the judge, and he said guilty as charged in nothin' flat and sentenced me to five years hard labor here for grand larceny! Ol' Luther . . . grinnin' from ear to ear, I gotta tell ya . . . come with the sheriff and his men this mornin' to . . ."

"Gibbs is still in town?" Buck asked sharply.

Moses shook his head. "Prob'ly not anymore. He prob'ly lit out pronto once all the rest of us was taken care of, and is headin' for the loot."

Fyffe automatically glanced at the northern office wall. "How long ago?"

McHugh answered for Moses. "Mr. Little was brought in about an hour or hour and a half ago. Takes that long to process a new inmate, as you know, Mr. Gi— uh . . ." He looked at the superintendent. "Ummm . . . what do you think, sir?"

The superintendent shook his head. He stared hard at Buck for a long moment, chewed a lip, stroked his beard, and preened his mustache. Fyffe waited tensely while the man scrutinized him; he knew that in prison stripes, filthy with dust plastered in his sweat, and in this location, he looked about the same at the moment as any other inmate. Still, he met the superintendent's eyes and tried to project quiet dignity.

Finally, the man said: "I'm not sure, Godfrey. This could be a plot to free Gibbs that went wrong for his gang, but . . . if he," he nodded at Fyffe, "is actually one of us in here by mistake . . ."

Buck said quickly: "I am, sir. I work for Lon— uh . . . Alonzo Humbert stationed in Prescott." Rapidly, he went on to tell the superintendent what had happened on the trail here, mentioned a few other officials—the Prescott sheriff, the judge, a couple of other high-ranking federal men—and finished: "If what Little says is true, Gibbs has only an hour or two head start. I may still be able to run him down and bring him back, but you have to let me out of here first."

The superintendent pondered that, frowning at both Buck and McHugh.

Desperately, Fyffe added to the turnkey: "You know Buckley Fyffe was the one who supposedly brought Luther Gibbs in, Mr. McHugh! The receipt you gave Luther proves it. Pete Roy out there recognized me, you saw that yourself! If you hold me now, two things will happen. Roy has probably already spread the word about who I am, and I'm dead by morning, and Luther Gibbs will live high off the hog on Southwestern's twenty-five thousand dollars, laughing all the way!"

Again, silence fell over the room. It was McHugh who finally broke it and clinched it for Buck. He murmured: "Sir, I think I believe him. I can't see four or five men getting themselves killed and one allowing himself to be sent here just to free their leader, no matter how loyal they are. I don't think this is Luther Gibbs. I think we are holding the wrong man."

The superintendent nodded, but still studied Fyffe closely.

Buck urged: "Sir, give me a horse and a weapon, let me out of here, and I'll bring that bastard in for you. I never lost a man before Gibbs, and he's not goin' to be my first."

"I'll do better than that," the superintendent said abruptly. "I'll give you clothing, a horse, weapons, money for trail supplies, and an Indian tracker. Mr. Lear, when will Chedan be back?"

The guard tipped his head. "He's down at the adobe yard right now, sir. Want me to go get him?"

"If you would, please." The superintendent didn't smile when he looked back at Buck. "Chedan isn't our tracker's real name, of course. It was given to him by his colleagues, Marshal

Fyffe . . . if you are Marshal Fyffe. Chedan is either the name of one of the Apache devils or their word for the devil, I've never been sure which. Suffice it to say that they claim he can track a fly blown past by the wind three days ago.

"We have several Apaches working for us who track escapees to claim the fifty-dollar-a-head reward we offer. Usually they return our charges alive, because they would have to carry a corpse, and Apaches don't like to touch a dead body, but sometimes they make an exception. Their reward is the same, dead or alive.

"If you are truly Marshal Fyffe, Chedan will help you track Luther Gibbs down and bring him here. If you are Luther Gibbs trying to pull a fast one on us, Chedan will discover it and will return you to us . . . one way or the other. Do you understand me?"

Buck nodded grimly. "I understand you, sir." He turned to Little. "Moses, Luther bragged to me that he told you boys where he cached the loot. Did he, really?"

The outlaw opened his mouth, but then looked at the other men in the room, and shut it.

"Come on, Moses," Buck snapped, "you want ol' Luther to get away with double-crossing you and to enjoy the money? Did he or didn't he tell you where he hid it?"

Again, Little glanced at the superintendent, at McHugh, and at the four guards before he said to Fyffe: "I tell you, Marshal, what do I get out of it? And I tell you in front of them, what makes you think you won't have half the guards from Yuma Prison hot on your tail, tryin' to beat you and Luther to the cache?" He shook his head. "Take me with you, Marshal. Yeah, Luther tol' us where he hid the money, but I sure as hell ain't gonna tell you . . . or them!"

"Perhaps a stint in the Snake Den would loosen his tongue, sir," one of the guards offered to the superintendent.

Buck cut in: "I can't wait that long. Gibbs is gettin' farther away every minute." He swung back to Little. "Moses, I'm not gonna take you with me, but wouldn't you like to be waitin' for ol' Luther when I bring him back? Wouldn't it give you a grin to see him in here breakin' rock right beside you instead of lollin' around San Francisco or the like, drinkin', whorin,' and gamin' up twenty-five thousand dollars you worked hard to get and your friends died for? At least tell me the general area, Moses!"

Little grimaced over a great howl of despair. He clasped both palms to his shaven skull for a moment before he choked: "Jerome! He hid the loot up near Jerome, but that's all he tol' us! That's the best I can do for you, Marshal."

"Good enough." Buck looked expectantly at the superintendent.

The man's eyes had slid past him toward the door, and Fyffe also turned in that direction. He saw the most dangerous-looking Apache he'd ever had the misfortune of meeting standing there with the guard Lear.

The superintendent said: "Come in, Chedan, and let me tell you what we have for you."

* * * * *

Out on the desert, Luther Gibbs rode Fyffe's horse and led a back-up mount burdened with supplies he had bought with Buck's money as he headed northeast. Smug over the recent turn of events, and complacent, he didn't realize he was being followed by a man on a roan mare and two companions who considered Buck Fyffe well-disposed of, so that now they had free rein with Luther Gibbs.

CHAPTER EIGHT

Chedan wore a white cloth headband to keep his heavy shoulder-length hair out of his eyes, a faded blue-figured calico shirt, baggy white cotton pants under a white cloth breechclout, and knee-high moccasins. Three lengths of leather wrapped his slim waist: a thin knife belt and a bullet-loaded gun belt slanted over a wide concho-decorated strip fastened in front with thongs rather than by a metal buckle. An amulet-weighted four-strand medicine cord passed diagonally across his chest beneath an unbuttoned brown vest. In his left hand, he carried a fine .44-40 Winchester rifle of the same kind the Yuma guards used; all-in-all, an odd mixture of Indian and white clothing and equipment both comfortable and functional.

The man himself was about five-feet eight-inches tall, and lightly built, almost like a boy in his teens, though Buck didn't think Chedan that young, maybe only a year or two less than himself. The features were distinctly Indian—high, prominent cheekbones, a strong nose and chin, and lips full but firm in a very dark, smooth face, but it was Chedan's eyes that tightened Fyffe's shoulders. They were hazel, not dark brown or black, holding more green than brown in their depths, and several shades lighter than the skin. Looking at those eyes, Buck thought: *No wonder they call him a devil!*

The superintendent said: "Thank you for coming, Chedan. This," he nodded at Buck, "is either Federal Marshal Buckley Fyffe in here by mistake, or the outlaw Luther Gibbs, rightfully incarcerated."

Buck watched the Apache's greenish eyes flick from the superintendent, to him, to Moses Little standing morosely among four guards, and back, while the superintendent explained the situation in detail and finished with: "Ordinary tracking and recapture reward is fifty dollars. For this job, I'll pay you a hundred. Will you accept the assignment?"

Buck noted that the superintendent was being uncommonly polite and courteous to the Apache; it gave him a real appreciation of the tracker's importance here.

Again, Chedan's strange eyes scrutinized Fyffe briefly before he nodded once and said in perfect English: "My pleasure."

"All right, good." The superintendent rose from his chair. "Do you want to take backup with you?"

Chedan's and Buck's eyes met and held for a moment before the Apache smiled slightly and shook his head. "No. I can handle him."

"He's bigger than you are, Chedan."

"But not as mean, sir."

"Your choice. Men, return Mr. Little to the compound. Godfrey, get Mr. Gibbs . . . or Marshal Fyffe . . . a bath, some civilian clothing, weapons, a mount, and trail supplies."

"Sir," McHugh frowned, "the only adequate animal we have in the corral at the moment is Barbarossa."

"Then he will have to do. Marshal Fyffe, I will see you again, either as Gibbs's corpse or as yourself bringing in your quarry. You are dismissed."

When the guards led him away, Little turned to Buck and snarled: "Bring Luther back, Marshal. I don't care about the money much anymore, but I want Gibbs in here with me! You bring him in, Marshal, you hear? You bring him in!"

"I'll do my best, Moses." Buck nodded. Tailed closely by Chedan, he followed McHugh out.

Buck took a quick bath. He was given clean underpants, a white shirt, black trousers and vest, a hat, bent-heel boots, an old but serviceable gun belt and sidearm, and a .44-40 Winchester complete with a goodly supply of ammunition. McHugh disappeared somewhere briefly, while Chedan kept his green gaze tight on Fyffe, and returned with a ten-dollar gold piece. He said: "This will buy supplies for your hunt."

Buck nodded again and pocketed the coin. "Thank you, Mr. McHugh. You're taking a lot on faith, here. I appreciate it."

McHugh didn't smile when he disagreed. "No, we're not. We're sending Chedan with you. If you are truly Marshal Fyffe, he will be a great help to you. If you're Luther Gibbs . . ." He shrugged. "Either case, you will be back. Come with me to the corral to get your mount."

The mount turned out to be the biggest, blackest mule Buck had ever seen, long-legged, at least six-feet tall at the shoulders, with a short scrubby tail, roached mane, and fire in his eye. Grinning broadly beneath his mustache, McHugh watched with Chedan and a couple of guards while Fyffe finally got Barbarossa cornered, bonneted, and saddled. When Buck was astride, he discovered the big mule willing, and that the critter moved with a softer gait than most horses.

The turnkey's parting words were: "Just don't touch his ears."

Buck nodded, responded: "I was raised in Virginia, Mr. McHugh. I'm well familiar with mules, thank you." He looked over at the Apache. "You ready to go, Chedan?"

"I'll catch up." The tracker whirled and dashed toward a dun pony lazing in the scant shade cast by the eastern wall of the stockade. Buck held Barbarossa steady while he watched the Indian leap into the saddle, catch reins, slide the rifle into its saddle scabbard, and whirl the horse toward him. He waited until Chedan arrived; he wasn't going to take off and have both the authorities still eyeing him suspiciously from various doorways, gates, and wall tops, and have the Apache say he had tried to escape at his first opportunity.

When he approached, Chedan grinned at Buck and made shooing motions with his right hand. He stayed slightly behind and to the left of Fyffe while they rode down the winding trail leading off the butte, then on into Yuma. Buck felt the Apache's look fastened to his spine as though the man had attached a rope to him, and it prickled what hair was growing out on the back of his neck. He didn't mention it, merely kept riding.

* * * * *

In town, Buck bought a bedroll, a water bag, and trail food. Sun hung low across the river when he tied everything to the back of his saddle and nodded to Chedan. "I'm ready. You need anything?"

"No. The land is bountiful."

"Okay, now you lead."

Chedan kicked his dun around and headed for the outskirts of town. Buck cast a quick look up at the prison painted in gold above free roofs at its feet, and shuddered. He wondered if he would again see the inside of that, and, if so, whether as a lawman or a returned escapee. Grimly, he yanked his eyes away, and now it was he who followed when Chedan led out of Yuma.

He urged Barbarossa up beside the Apache's pony and said:

"I think Gibbs may be riding my horse. If yes, I can tell you that I had new shoes put on him at Umbrite's just before we left Prescott. Henry Umbrite guarantees his work and marks all shoes he makes with an 'HU' so nobody can claim that some shoddy work was his doings. If Gibbs still has my horse, the shoe prints will be distinct."

Chedan nodded but said nothing. He had started his sweep back at the prison trail and now leaned out of the saddle to search the ground. Presently, he pointed. "Like that?"

Buck nudged Barbarossa closer and also scowled at the sign impressed into the dirt. "Yep. Like that."

"*Hau*," Chedan breathed. Instead of immediately following the hoofprints, he turned his mount east along the butte's rock face, then, walked the dun some quarter mile out into the flat.

"What are you doin'?" Buck frowned.

"Too many men, horses, and wagons travel near the prison and town. Gibbs has several ways to get back to Jerome . . . He could have gone into Yuma and is waiting in a room there for the next boat upriver to Ehrenberg, then to take the road to Prescott and Jerome from the south . . . or he can ride the boat to Fort Mojave and come in from the north or west. He might go by horseback up the road between here and northern campos, or he might lite out across country. Now that I know what I'm lookin' for, I can find out whether he ever left town. Useless to hunt for a man in the desert when he's sittin' and drinkin' in a saloon."

That makes sense, Buck thought. He had done a lot of man hunting himself, but this Apache probably knew twice as much about tracking as he did, and it behooved him to learn from an expert.

Some ten minutes later, Chedan said: "There he went."

Buck scowled at a track nearly obliterated by those of three horses overlaying the crescent marked "HU." "He has others with him. That doesn't make sense! All his men were either gunned-down or put in prison."

Chedan shook his head. "I don't think they are with him, I think they passed by later."

"Just goin' the same way?"

"Followin' him."

"Really! Guards from the prison?"

"Uhn-uh. They came from town. And Gibbs is leadin' a green packhorse . . . See here?" Chedan's finger indicated other hoof prints beside the ones marked "HU." "That animal don't like bein' led. He's crabbin' along. Well, you ready, we'll follow them that's followin' Gibbs. You don't know who they are?"

"Not the slightest idea. How far ahead are they?"

"'Bout two hours."

"Then, we've got some ridin' to do to catch up. Lead on."

The Apache nodded. He paused a moment to untie his concho belt, removed it, and stashed it in his saddlebags. He saw Fyffe's curious look and grinned faintly. "Don't want sun flashing off silver to give us away."

"You like what you do, don't you?"

"That, I do."

"Any reason in particular . . . besides the money?"

Chedan's smile broadened. It made him look to Buck like an evil teenager. "It keeps me off the reservation. Besides, it's the only job I know of where the white man pays me to hunt other white men."

"And kill them?"

"Sometimes."

"Uh . . . you lookin' to kill me?"

"That depends on who you really are." Chedan urged his mount forward.

Well, Buck thought, *at least there is no doubt about where I stand with the Apache.* If he couldn't prove to Chedan's satisfaction that he was who he was, he was probably dead, unless he killed the devil first. His problem was, he needed Chedan's help in this, which meant he would have to wait as long as was safe, then try to defend himself come some kind of attack.

An hour later, as the sun became perched atop far mountain peaks in California, the Apache slowed his horse, leaned out of the saddle to scowl at the ground, and grunted: "Huh."

Buck reined in. "What?"

"How many men you say brought you to Yuma?"

"Two. Luther Gibbs and Cecil Clapp. The rest headed straight into town. Why?"

Chedan straightened and stared narrow-eyed around the darkling land. "'Cause we just crossed sign of the same riders followin' three horses that way . . . " His thumb jerked southwest. " . . . and now follow that way." He nodded forward. "Those same men been followin' for a long time."

"How can you tell? That was almost a week ago!"

"Been no rain. No heavy wind." Chedan's eyes flared green in the fading light when he looked over at Fyffe. "Tracks are still here. You sure you don't know who those three riders are?"

"No, I don't, but I'm sure as hell goin' to find out . . . though not tonight. We're still too close to Yuma. We got time."

Together, he and Chedan rode on, following those who followed Luther Gibbs.

* * * * *

Several things happened at the prison that day and night. Pete Roy reached the end of his sixty-day punishment, and the ball and chain was removed from his ankle with a stern admonishment from the turnkey, McHugh, for better behavior. Roy held a conversation with the guard, McNair, as to what had become of Luther Gibbs . . . or Marshal Buckley Fyffe . . . and heard about the release.

Later that evening, Pete escaped his cell, killed a guard walking the top of the finished portion of the wall, exchanged his prison garb for the guard's uniform, dumped the body beside a pile of bricks, hastily covered it with loose adobe rectangles, and walked the man's beat for five minutes or so until he was sure no one had become alarmed.

With the pistol belted around his hips and the Winchester in hand, he slithered down the unfinished portion of the wall and left. Keeping to the shadows, he made his way into Yuma. He had found scant money in the guard's pockets, but enough to legitimately buy a few trail supplies. What he couldn't buy, he would steal, and then Buck Fyffe had better watch his back, because he, Pete Roy, was out for revenge.

Meanwhile, Moses Little died in the Snake Den. Joe McNair and Harold Johnson, two of the guards who had taken him and Buck to the superintendent's office, had there heard the tale of the twenty-five thousand stashed up in the Jerome area, and wanted to know more. They hauled Moses into the cavern, shut but didn't lock the two metal doors to muffle light and sound, chained Little to the cage grill, and proceeded to ask him exactly where Gibbs had told him the loot was hidden.

Eventually, Little talked. By the time Johnson slid a knife into his heart, Moses was so far gone that the coup de grace was almost redundant, but at least it released him from the pain of sinuses cleared with a candle flame held under his nose.

The guards took away the manacles, left Moses where he lay, shut the iron doors behind them when they left, and were confident that no one would discover the body until the next inmate got himself into enough trouble to be sentenced there. By that time, they would be long gone.

Presently, Yuma Prison was short three employees and two inmates.

CHAPTER NINE

"Boy, I don't know," Buck murmured barely above a whisper, "but I think those were about the best damned beans I ever ate."

He and Chedan had followed hoofprints until it became too dark to see. They stopped for the night and dry-camped without lighting a night fire because the moon was up; it and the stars gave them enough light for what little they did to settle in, and they didn't want to betray their presence to those they tracked.

Once, the Apache stood upright on his pony's back to scrutinize the desert. When he leaped down to the ground, he said to Fyffe: "One fire three or four miles north. Prob'ly Gibbs. The men trailin' him are also dark-campin', unless they found a hole to hide their fire."

"Well, if Luther is just moseyin' along, we should catch up with him tomorrow." It was then that Buck got a can of beans from his supplies, opened the tin with his knife, and ate the contents cold. He finished the beans with a final: "Mmmm . . . yeah!"

Chedan's teeth were a white slash in the night when he grinned before he said: "More likely it's because those beans aren't laced with saltpeter."

Fyffe scowled up at the Apache from where he sat cross-legged on the ground in the tiny cactus-surrounded clearing. "What?"

"Saltpeter," Chedan repeated. "Couldn't you taste it in the prison food?"

"Uh . . . yeah, the vittles tasted awful, but I thought it was that muddy water that caused it."

"Saltpeter," Chedan said again. "They put it in the inmates' food to suppress their carnal urges." He took items Buck couldn't define in the darkness from out of his saddlebags, also settled to the sand, and began to eat.

Recalling Burnside, Buck thought the saltpeter didn't do a lot toward suppressing carnal urges . . . Knuckles in the teeth were more effective. But the Apache's phrasing brought up another subject. "Chedan, where'd you learn to speak English so well?"

"The Society of Friends. The Quakers. When I was a young'un, my father sent me over into New Mexico to where they had opened a school for Mescaleros. The Quakers cut my hair, dressed me in white man's clothing, and taught me English and farming . . . tried to teach me farming. I am a warrior, not a farmer."

"And not Mescalero?"

"White Mountain. I am White Mountain."

"But you surely learned our language well."

"My father said that in order to really know the enemy, you had to speak his tongue."

Buck tensed. He set the empty bean tin on the sand and reached for the piece of charqui he'd laid on his knee. "You think us whites are your enemies?"

"Aren't you?"

Fyffe could see this conversation moving in a dangerous direction and tried to change the subject. He commented: "I didn't know the Quakers were out here. I thought it was mostly Spanish Catholic or Mormon."

"Oh, yes. By now, they have more than a dozen agency schools set up around the land. I originally learned English full of thees and thous. Had to unlearn that."

"Humph. Uh . . . your family is still east of here? You get to see them often?"

"Not as often as I would like. Every six months or so, is all. But my wife is a virtuous woman who waits for me. She knows I have become wise in your ways and get rich by hunting white men for white men." Again, Chedan's teeth gleamed to a grin. "Who knows? One day, I may lead my people in the battle to reclaim our lands from you. Then, my sons will follow me back into our true paths."

Buck let that go. He asked: "Sons? How many?"

"Three. And a daughter. You have a wife and sons?"

"Not anymore."

"Not home often enough to hold them to you?"

"Dead of typhoid."

"Hau."

Buck scowled. "I thought 'hau' meant 'good' or 'good peace.' You sayin' 'good' that my wife and daughter died?"

"Yes. Now, I won't have the problem one day in the future of perhaps having to kill the family of somebody I know. Killing strangers is one thing. Killing neighbors . . . maybe friends . . . that's another. Are you gonna just run Luther Gibbs down tomorrow and haul him back to Yuma?"

Buck paused a long moment, thinking about that before he answered. "No. First off, I want to find out who those three men are you say been taggin' along both comin' and goin'. Then, I plan to follow Gibbs clean on into Jerome. We never did find the stolen money . . . He wouldn't tell where it was durin' his trial up in Prescott, and all Moses Little said was that the loot was hidden at Jerome, but not where there. I want to get both Luther and the money back, and then the slate will be clean all around."

"And you get a big reward."

"No." Buck shook his head. "Federal marshals can't claim a reward. It's our job to bring in miscreants. We get paid a salary, and that's it."

"Well, then, maybe I can claim the reward, if there is one."

"There is. Southwestern is offerin' five thousand dollars for return of their twenty-five." Buck finished the jerky, drank from his water bag, rose, and got his bedroll from his saddle. "Get some sleep, Chedan. I want to be up and movin' on by dawn."

* * * * *

With the fall of darkness, Luther's elation began to wear off. For the first time, he realized he was alone out here in the vast, empty Sonoran desert. He huddled close to his little fire, listening to sounds he couldn't identify, feeling eyes he didn't know watching him from somewhere. Behind him. He drew Buck Fyffe's sidearm and shifted to the other side of the fire. Shifted again. And again. Always, the eyes were behind him.

His own eyes flicking here and there at the darkness, he clutched the pistol with a sweaty hand and breathed more than sang: "Oh, Susanna, don't you cry for me . . . I'm goin' north to Jerome, my money for to see . . ."

* * * * *

In the brush ever-thickening as they proceeded northward, one watcher lowered his binoculars and grinned at his companion.

"He's spooked. Serves the bastard right. But that gives me an idea."

They kept up their surveillance during the night. They didn't know that they themselves were being tracked.

* * * * *

Early in the morning, barely after first dawn light, the paddle-wheel steamer, Colonel Stanton, one of the riverboats owned by the Colorado Steam Navigation Company, loaded supplies both civilian and military, and began its journey upriver from Yuma toward Fort Mojave. Pete Roy made it aboard just as they pulled in the gangplank. Still dressed in the guard's uniform, armed with the dead man's pistol, and carrying the Winchester, he put on an Irish accent and asked the deckhand how much the fare was to Hardyville, gasping breathlessly: "I just got a letter from me sis there that me poor ol' mither was dyin'. Three weeks on the road that correspondence was! I might already be too late to say goodbye, but . . . saints presarve me . . . I'm gonna at least try to make me mither's wake and funeral!"

It was almost wasted effort. The deckhand was a Mexican who understood very little English. In response, he told Pete: "See jefe. I know nada. See jefe." He jabbed a thumb up toward the pilothouse.

"Yeah. Thanks." Roy headed around the deck to the California side of the ship, but, when near the bow, flattened himself suddenly against the cabin wall, because two other men dressed in Yuma prison guards' uniforms were already there leaning on the rail. He recognized Joe McNair and Harold Johnson. What the hell were they doing here?

The only other passengers on board seemed to be a young couple not fully awake who sat on one of the benches near the cabin wall, and a boy about nine or ten clutching a salt sack that may have held food. There was a paper pinned to his shirt announcing: E'BERG. He perched on a rope coil and looked at Roy with dark, wary eyes. He appeared to be terrified to be alone here, and didn't say anything.

Pete nodded to the boy before he looked at the land passing on their right. The captain had moved the ship toward mid-river but not into the central current, and the thrash of the stern wheel and chug of engines nearly overrode a faint wail of alarm pursuing them from atop Prison Hill.

Roy smiled thinly. The authorities had discovered him gone. He could picture a guard winding the siren handle while other guards and the super and turnkey ran this way and that looking for him. They would call in the Indians to track him. Let them. His footprints may lead from the prison on into town, but there they would become lost among those of the locals, and river water retained no spoor.

Rifle in his left hand, he leaned to peer around the cabin corner and frowned. McNair was alone. Where had Johnson gone? With a cold glance at the little boy who still eyed him, he pushed away from the wall and sauntered toward the stern. He found Johnson pressed against the railing, peeing into foam splashed up by the big paddle wheel. With a quick look around to ensure privacy, he stepped up behind Johnson, slammed a fist against the back of the man's neck, and caught his victim by the jacket when Harold collapsed unconscious.

Another glance around told Roy they were still alone. Quickly, he lay his Winchester on the deck, searched the guard's clothing, and came up with a handful of money he didn't bother to count before he jammed it into his own pockets. He ignored the loaded gun belt, but found half a passage ticket. He tucked that into his pocket along with the greenbacks.

By this time, Harold was beginning to wake up. Pete hit him again, twice. He tossed Johnson's .44-40 overboard, slid the man to the side, eased him gently over the rail beside the churning paddle wheel and dropped him. The edge of a paddle caught Harold's coattail. Arms and legs flopping wildly, Johnson went around with the wheel once before he vanished for good under the brown, silt-thick water.

Roy turned to look down the length of the ship. The little boy, knees drawn up to his chest, the salt sack clutched tightly and eyes huge over a mouth opened in shock, stared at him. Pete picked up his own shoulder weapon, pointed it at the child, and mouthed a silent *pow!* He sent a warning glare at the boy and pressed a finger against his lips to tell the kid to keep quiet.

The boy's mouth shut. He crouched lower over his knees and looked at the deck.

Pete grinned and moved toward the bow. He had money, weapons, and proof of purchased passage; now, to take care of Joe McNair. Unbuttoning his jacket, he drew his sidearm. The Winchester again in his left hand, he folded his arms across his chest so the cocked pistol was hidden under one side of his coat front. His grin broadened when he passed the boy and waggled brows at him. Still seated on the rope coil, the child swiveled around, grabbed the middle safety rail, rested his chin on the back of his hand, and stared intently at water turbid beside the hull.

Roy chuckled. He walked up beside McNair, moved to the rail next to the guard, and pressed the pistol barrel into Joe's ribs. When McNair darted a surprised glance at him, he said: "Hiya, Mr. McNair."

Joe raised his right arm to peer down at jacket material jammed against him, then, mouth open, up at Pete. He choked: "Roy! J-Jesus Christ, what are you doin' here? H-How . . .?"

"Keep it down, McNair. Just hang on to your hair. Drop

your rifle into the river. Do it!" When Joe let the .44-40 fall into brown water, Pete nodded. "Now, we're gonna take a quiet-like stroll toward the back of this here tub, right? One wrong move outta you, and you're a goner, you understand me? We got things to discuss, so just walk quiet and nice, right?"

McNair's eyes shuttled around what deck was visible. Again, Pete laughed. "You lookin' for ol' Harold, he's feedin' the fish, but you and me, we got business to take care of. Move it!"

McNair moved. On the bench in the shade, the young wife slept with her head on her man's shoulder. The husband stared vacantly toward California and gave no notice to the two men in uniform as they passed. Across the deck, the little boy turned his head but not his body to peer under his arm at them, then quickly looked away. Those who manned the steamer were below tending engines and doing whatever else occupied them. The captain was also the pilot busy watching for drifting trees and other dangerous debris that might foul the paddle wheel, and Pete had McNair and the deck mostly to himself.

He said: "Stop here, Joe. I want to hear all about how come you and Harold just happen to be aboard the Colonel Stanton."

"Uh . . . v-vacation! Time off! Uh . . ."

"Like hell." Roy pressed the pistol harder into McNair's rib cage. "Give me a straight answer . . . now."

Joe went ashen when he looked at Pete. He gasped: "Did anybody ever tell you your eyes look like they belong to a sick rat?"

"Nobody who lived to say it twice. Now lissen to me. Only a scrawny Messican seen me come on board, and he don't count. I got ol' Johnson's passage ticket stub to prove I paid fare. For appearance's sake, I'd prefer that two Yuma guards got on this washtub and two get off, but that don't mean you can't suffer a serious accident sometime durin' the dark of night, y'know?

"Now, me, I'm looking to get my hands on Buck Fyffe. First

few days till that new loser came into Yuma, ol' Marshal Fyffe said he was somebody called Gibbs. Why was he in there as Gibbs, eh? You explain it all to me, Joe." Roy twitched the pistol.

"Y-You wouldn't shoot me here in broad daylight, with everybody watchin', Pete. You'd never g-get away with . . ."

"I done ol' Johnson in broad daylight with ever'body watchin' and no one knowin' the difference, Joe. I expect ol' Harold is passin' the Narrows about now, on his way to Mexico. You won't be any more trouble a'tall. Talk to me!"

McNair talked in almost the same tone Moses Little had used before his demise. Roy listened without comment until the guard was finished, then grinned and holstered the pistol.

"You done good, Joe. Lemme tell you what we got, here. I want Fyffe. You want Gibbs's big take. You say Buck and that Injun are trailin' this Luther Gibbs to the cache, maybe. You and me, we'll go to Jerome, too. I get Fyffe . . . you get the money, then we go our separate ways, and ever'body's happy, except ol' Buck, who is gonna be dead, ol' Gibbs, who is gonna be dead and broke, and maybe that Injun as a side deal. We're pardners, Joe. You and me, we're pardners. You got too much on me and I got too much on you for either of us to double-cross the other. So . . ." Out of the corner of his eye, he saw the boy leave his rope coil and move closer to the young couple. The kid wasn't talking to them, merely being near them. He pondered that situation for a silent moment before he finished: "Relax, Joe. Now, we're in this together."

"Yeah, Pete," McNair gulped. "Partners. Together. All the way, Pete. No question about it."

They lounged quietly on the deck in whatever shade was available, Pete Roy watching McNair and the little boy alternately, Joe trying without success to relax. Late in the afternoon, the paddle-wheeler pulled in to shore at the end of a long single-wide two-by-twelve plank pier supported by rickety pole pilings. The boat paused only long enough to let the young couple step from the deck to the planks. The wheel continued to turn to hold the steamer steady against the current; when the couple was offloaded, bells rang, there was a shift of gears, the Colonel Stanton drifted backward for a moment, then smoke and steam puffed, and the ship resumed its labored churn upriver.

Roy looked at the barren mountainous land at the east and muttered: "Gawd, I wonder where them two are headed? Ain't nothin' there I can see but Injuns, cactus, rocks, and . . . nothin'."

"Wouldn't know." Joe was afraid not to give some kind of an answer. At sundown, he would become more afraid.

The little boy sat on the bench the couple had vacated. He opened his salt sack, pulled out a greasy brown-paper package, and opened it to expose half a baked chicken. Head lowered and eyes warily on the two uniformed men at ease near the stern, he began to eat. Another paper package produced cookies half crumbled from his past clutch.

Pete watched the child watch him, and continued to wait. The stern-wheeler was again out near midstream. When he saw the boy carefully wrap what remained of his supplies in paper and stash the leftovers back in the sack, he said to McNair: "You set. I'm goin' to stretch my legs." He rose, sauntered around the other side of the double-decker cabins, and yawned. He was hungry, but his many visits to the Snake Den and living for days on bread and muddy water had accustomed him to that. He rounded the front cabin in time to see the boy lean off the bench and peer toward where he had been.

"Lookin' for me?"

White-faced, the child jerked around to stare up at him.

Pete nodded. "You done good, boy. Kept your mouth shut. That was wise of you. What's your name?"

"I . . . ain't s'posed to talk to strangers," the boy said in a low voice.

"Oh, hell, I ain't exactly a stranger, now, am I? I mean, after all, we share a real big secret, don't we? You figger we should let that hombre down there in on it?"

The boy automatically looked to where Joe McNair still sat. Roy reached out, slapped a hand over the child's face, pinched the nose between thumb and forefinger, sealed the mouth with his palm, and with his other arm, captured the boy's arms to draw the kid to him. He sat down on the bench, flung a leg over the boy's to subdue the kicking, and stared blankly out at California passing at the west as though he disassociated himself from what he was doing.

He held until the child stopped struggling and went limp, and continued to hold a few moments longer to make sure before he rose, carried the body to the rail, and, as he had with Harold Johnson, eased the corpse into the river so it wouldn't splash.

In the stern, some faint sound had drawn McNair's attention. He crouched on all fours staring open-mouthed at Roy. When Pete returned to the bench, sat, and picked up the boy's salt sack, Joe scrambled to his feet and stumbled toward his "partner." He pointed a finger at the water and gasped: "He was only a kid . . . a little . . . You . . . he . . . you didn't . . . shouldn't . . . He was only a little kid!"

"Good," Roy said, unwrapping the package. "There's some chicken left."

McNair lunged for the rail and threw up. He had never feared any man before in his life like he feared Roy.

Pete grinned. Before biting into the chicken, he said: "Sick, eh? Well, guess you won't want any of this, then."

CHAPTER TEN

Three hard-ridden days since leaving Yuma, when Gibbs reached the wagon and stagecoach road between Ehrenberg and Prescott, he turned eastward onto it. The early start that Buck and Chedan had gotten that first morning had let them catch up with Luther and his shadows, but after they neared, they kept well out into the brush and behind the others, merely following along close enough not to lose their quarry, but far enough aside and to the rear not to be noticed.

This day passed relatively uneventfully until late afternoon, and then things took a turn for the bizarre for Buck. He and Chedan were in the brush on the south side of the road. The three unknown followers had crossed to the north side some-time in the dark, but now two of them, one on a roan mare and one riding a bay, broke from the brush back out onto the road. They headed openly toward Gibbs at a fast enough pace to overtake him but not at such a clip that it would appear they ran him down.

Luther Gibbs heard them coming first, scowled over his shoulder at his back trail, then reined his mount around to face the strangers. He hauled his packhorse to a halt and waited, his palm on his gun butt.

In the southern brush, Buck and Chedan drew up opposite Gibbs, dismounted, and edged silently toward the road. The Apache murmured: "Careful. That third man is still out there somewhere."

Buck nodded. Narrow-eyed, he hunkered down behind a mesquite to watch and listen, but then his mouth fell open and his fingers closed so hard on the Apache's arm that Chedan nearly tried to jerk away. Green eyes wide with surprise, the tracker glanced from the three men on the road to his companion in time to see all blood drain out of Fyffe's face before it flashed back to a flush of surprise and perhaps rage.

Neither of them said anything, because out on the road, the two men slowed their horses to a walk, and the one on the roan lifted both hands empty into the air.

"Hold on, hombre, we don't mean you no harm. We're just passin' along from Ehrenberg up to the highlands. Just takin' the same road. If you let us by, we'll mosey on."

Luther didn't move fingers from his weapon. "Goin' to what highlands?"

"Up through Prescott and on to Jerome. I got mining interests there, and Felix here, he's heard there may be a famous calico queen livin' there that he's hankerin' to meet. So, if you don't mind . . ."

Gibbs's eyes narrowed another notch. "Jerome? You're headed for Jerome?"

The man on the roan lowered his arms to take up the reins. "That's what I said. Uh . . . my name's Jack Stone. This here's Felix Smith. Who might you be?"

Luther eyed the newcomers. The man on the mare who called himself Stone was maybe six-feet tall, florid-faced, with brown eyes and a French-style waxed light-brown mustache. Felix Smith appeared short, wiry, sun-weathered, and blue-eyed, with dark brown hair. He was clean-shaven but stubbled. He obviously hadn't smoothed his cheeks in a couple of days.

Gibbs said quickly: "Marshal Buckley Fyffe, stationed in Prescott."

"Oh, now, right proud to meet up with you, Marshal." Stone smiled. He tipped a finger to his hat brim. "Y'all have a safe journey, sir." He urged his mare around Gibbs. Felix touched his own hat brim, nodded to Luther, and followed.

"Wait!" Gibbs called. "Uh . . . hold up, there. Uh . . . since we're all goin' the same direction, would you mind me ridin' along with you boys? This here is dangerous country for a man alone. Safety in numbers and like that, y'know."

Stone slowed his roan and grinned back at Luther. "No, not at all. In fact, it'd be a comfort to us to have a lawman along. You also comin' out of Ehrenberg?"

"No, Yuma." Gibbs kicked his mount into motion to join the two strangers. Together, their horses held to an easy, mile-eating canter, the three of them moved on eastward.

In the brush, Buck crouched frozen and watched them go. Across the road, that third man and his horse flitted from mesquite to tamarisk to clump of prickly pear as he followed.

Still, Fyffe sat unmoving, blue eyes bleak in an expression drawn with disbelief.

Chedan finally pried his arm from fingers Buck seemed unable to open. "You know those men, don't you. What the hell's the matter with you, Fyffe?"

Buck said: "Josh Stoner."

"No, he said Jack Stone. And the other one is . . ."

"No! Not Jack Stone. Federal Marshal Joshua Stoner out of Santa Fe, New Mexico. He was in Prescott when Steve Larson and I left with Luther . . . He'd brought Gus Parker in for murder." He turned his head slowly toward the Apache. "And that's not Felix Smith, that's Felix Glover. He is a Southwestern security man. I worked with him and his partner, Gilbert Root, to track Luther the first time. We . . . we got separated over by Camp Verde. Root and I were the ones who ran across Luther. I'll bet he . . . Gibbs . . . never saw Glover. I know he doesn't know Stoner is law. But that . . . that means . . ."

"That the third man still trailin' them is Root?"

"What the hell is goin' on here? I got to find out what's goin' on!" Buck leaped up to a half crouch and bolted back to where Barbarossa and Chedan's pony were tethered. Bemused, the Apache followed.

* * * * *

Luther Gibbs, Josh Stoner, and Felix Glover kept to the road the rest of the day, moving on not particularly fast, but steadily. Buck and Chedan crossed the road to be on the same side as that third man, and trailed him at a discreet distance. Buck only waited until nightfall, and then he intended to get some answers.

Luther, Stoner, and Felix halted at sundown and made camp in the brush on the north side of the road. The shadower also halted. He buried himself deep in a shield of mesquite and cactus, dug a hole with his knife, mounded the sand up around the edges, and built a tiny fire in the bottom. He kept the blaze small enough that its light wouldn't show above the rim and proceeded to cook his dinner.

To the west of him, Fyffe and Chedan halted their mounts and settled down to wait. Buck opened another can of beans, supplemented them with jerky and water, finished his meal with a warm, nearly-withered apple, and stared grimly into the building darkness while Chedan ate of the oddities he carried in his own bags.

Neither of them said anything. Whatever occupied the Indian's brain, Buck's thoughts were in turmoil. He didn't want to believe in what he thought had happened, but even as his mind and heart rejected it, his instincts knew it was true. He tried his best to argue himself out of it, told himself not to make snap judgments, that things couldn't possibly be how they appeared on the surface, and that he had to wait to see who that trailing man was and what he had to say before he made any kind of solid assessment of the situation. Still, his gut seethed with the certain knowledge of what he was going to discover.

Chedan asked quietly: "What do you intend to do with the follower after we question him? It wouldn't be wise to let him run loose."

"Tie him up and take him with us," Buck said shortly. "Nothin' else to do."

Chedan let that go. He rose to stash the remains of his meal back in his saddlebags, then returned to squat on his heels by Fyffe. "I've got manacles in my carry-sacks in case you need them."

"You do?" Buck was surprised.

"Sure. How do you think you're goin' back to Yuma if you turn out to be Luther Gibbs instead of Buck Fyffe? I come prepared."

Buck breathed a soft, morose laugh. "Yeah, well, if you're ready, let's go keep a closer eye on that gent over yonder."

They left Barbarossa and Chedan's pony tethered to bushes and slipped silently toward the miniscule glow cast by the follower's little night fire. They lay hidden in the clearing edge brush and watched the man finish his coffee, smoke a thin, bent Mexican cheroot, check his weaponry for load, then roll himself in a blanket. With one hand near his rifle, he glanced warily around before he sighed heavily and shut his eyes. They continued to wait until the man's breathing and an occasional snore announced he was asleep, then rose and moved into the area.

Buck drew his pistol, stepped forward quickly, squatted, and jammed the barrel under the man's nose. Chedan stood a short distance to the right, his own weapon drawn and aimed. When Root's eyes and mouth flew open, Fyffe smiled grimly and said: "Hello, Gil. Fancy meetin' you here. Not one sound till I tell you to talk, then you'd better have a lot to say."

Root didn't move other than that his eyes shuttled between the pistol under his nose, the Indian off to the side, and Fyffe, while the latter yanked the blanket from around him and relieved him of his sidearm. A pistol in each hand, Fyffe rose, stepped over, and kicked the rifle out of Root's reach before he again squatted, this time beside the dying fire.

"Now, you can get up, Gil."

Root only pushed himself up onto his elbows. His eyes darted to Chedan briefly before he looked back at the white man and gasped: "Wh-Who are you! How d'you know me? What call you got to . . . ?"

Buck's brows rose. "You don't know me?"

"N-No. I got no money . . . nothin' you can take me for. Only a few vittles and some water. You can have that, if you want, but . . ."

Fyffe was astonished; he wouldn't have thought a beard and a little dirt would alter his appearance that much. He cut Root off with: "I'm Buck Fyffe, Gil."

"B-Buck? Fyffe? Fyffe? Why ain't you in Y-Yuma Prison?"

"They paroled me for good behavior," Buck snapped. "Tell me what you're doin' here, Gil, why Josh and Felix are ridin' with Luther Gibbs at the moment, and how you knew I was in Yuma."

Root looked back at Chedan. The Apache grinned at him, but it wasn't the kind of smile that instilled a lot of comfort in anyone. "Who the hell is that?"

"That is Chedan, a real good friend of mine, Gil. I been told that 'chedan' means devil in his language, and that his own people named him that. Answer my questions."

Gil licked lips. He pushed himself up to sit, and nodded to Fyffe. "Glad to tell you, Buck. I never liked this operation from the outset, anyway, but I was ordered to it. Uh . . . when ol' Luther Gibbs refused to say where our money was hidden, Wally Lake . . ."

"Your boss at Southwestern?"

"Yeah. Head of security there. Lake got together with your boss, Lon Humbert, and they cooked up a plan to get our money back. Humbert assigned you and Steve Larson to escort Gibbs to Yuma, and Marshal Stoner to go along with me and Felix Glover, to trail you."

"All the way from Prescott," Buck said bluntly. He could feel rage building inside him. He knew what was coming, but had to hear Root say it aloud.

"Yeah," Gil went on. "Our job was to see that Luther escaped you before you and Steve could get him to prison, because Lake and Humbert figgered Luther would head straight for the loot, and we could track him and get our money back . . ."

"So, you merely slunk along out in the brush and watched while Steve died."

"Uh . . . yeah. He . . . the reason Humbert picked Larson was because he had the lung fever. He was a lunger who wouldn't have lived much longer anyway, and . . . besides, what could we do about a rattler strike?"

"Never mind that Steve had a wife and children."

"Yeah, well, maybe his wife got done a favor, y'know?

Now, she don't have to set and watch him wither away with the lung fever."

"And when the Gibbs gang attacked me, you merely looked on and didn't help me."

"Well, yeah, uh . . . yeah."

"You expected them to find Luther and me, kill me and rescue Luther while you merely sat with your thumbs up your asses and watched? Why didn't Lon let Steve and me in on the plan?"

"Uh . . . Humbert said you'd never go for it, 'cause you're too straight arrow. But he said that since you din't have a wife . . . no family . . ."

"I am . . . disposable? You're tellin' me that my own boss, the man I've worked with . . . worked under . . . have called friend for years ordered this? Lon set Steve and me up to . . ."

"Well, you ain't got no wife or kids, and Larson, he was dyin' anyway! When Wally Lake came to Humbert with the proposal, they agreed it was a good idea, a way they would never have otherwise to locate Southwestern's stolen money, and they had to assign somebody to take Gibbs to Yuma."

"And when I escaped Gibbs and his men, you just stood by and watched them hunt me down and drag me back?"

Again, Root shot a glance at Chedan listening silently with his pistol still aimed steadily at him, before he swallowed hard, and nodded.

"And when Luther and Cecil Clapp delivered me to Yuma as Luther, I'll bet you 'bout jumped for joy!"

"Uh . . . no, but we . . . I mean, we were glad they din't kill you, but . . ."

"But you were willin' to let me spend fifteen years inside prison walls in Gibbs's place so he could go free and lead you to the money. Twenty-five thousand dollars! By God, I don't come cheap, I'll give you that!

"What did you plan to do had Steve not got snakebit and Luther's boys hadn't caught up with us and rescued him before Larson and I could get Gibbs to Yuma?" Buck's voice had softened to a dangerous hiss. "Tell me what you were gonna do then, Gilbert."

"We were goin' to h-have to . . . take our own steps to free Gibbs."

"In other words, you were goin' to kill Steve. Ambush me."

"Uh . . . no . . . uh . . . well, yeah, but . . ."

Chedan's eyes narrowed when Fyffe dropped the pistols and breathed: "My own boss ordered it? I'm a lawman! I've spent eleven years upholdin' the law, and now you say my own boss ordered me killed? My friend, Josh Stoner, a man I've worked with more than a couple of times in the past, was gonna pull the trigger on me just so Southwestern could get back their damned money?"

"Buck . . ." Chedan began, but Fyffe sprang at Root, wrapped both hands around the man's neck, and bore Gil to the sand.

Buck grated: "Willin' to let me spend fifteen years in Yuma just to get back your gawddamned money?"

"Buck!" Chedan jammed his weapon back into its holster, leaped on Fyffe's back, and tried to pry his fingers from Root's throat, but the marshal was bigger than he was, outrage lent him strength, and he couldn't budge him.

"Disposable?" Buck howled. He squeezed until cords stood out in his own neck. Veins were blue worms in his temples. Root clawed at him without effect. Chedan couldn't dislodge him.

"Steve's and my lives worth less than your precious money? Sent us only 'cause he was sick and my wife is dead? Years and years behind bars in some hellhole just because . . ."

Something hit Fyffe hard across the back of the skull.

Without a sound, his hands still locked to Gill's neck, he collapsed to the sand beside Root.

* * * * *

When Buck came around, the first thing he saw was Chedan squatted beside the little fire, thoughtfully tossing broken twigs into the flames. He started to put a hand to his aching head. It was then that he discovered his wrists locked behind him with iron manacles, that a length of leather bound his ankles, and that a cloth between his teeth and knotted behind his head effectively gagged him.

He squirmed to sit up, and with that motion, another figure caught his attention. Gilbert Root lay on his back. His eyes stared at the stars. His throat looked like a whore's rouged lips opened beneath his chin.

Chedan noted that Fyffe had come to and was scowling at Root's corpse. He said softly: "Tried to escape. Couldn't have him warning the others about us.

"Now, Buck, you lay there and listen to me for a minute." When Fyffe's eyes shifted to him, he went on. "I now believe you're who you say you are. You are Buckley Fyffe, not Luther Gibbs. He," he nodded at Root's body, "confirmed it. But I'm gonna leave you trussed-up till you get yourself together. You have a right to feel betrayed. I understand your anger . . . No Apache would ever do a brother like your own have done you, and I feel your outrage. But you damned near gave us away with your shoutin'. In fact, I figger those three yonder must not have posted a night guard else they'd have heard you and come to see what the hell was goin' on here.

"So, I tell you, you stay like you are till I'm sure you got a good hold on yourself. The more you struggle, the longer I leave the chains and the gag on. Understand?"

Buck nodded. He stopped trying to sit up, went limp, and shut his eyes. Teeth clamped against the cloth between them, he searched for answers to what he should do now.

Laurie, dammit, Laurie, help me . . .

He felt tears burning behind closed lids and fought them down. They were from fury and betrayal, but he knew Chedan would see them as a sign of weakness, and he couldn't have that.

"You gonna make a fuss if I take away the gag?"

Buck kept his eyes shut but shook his head.

"You start yellin' again, I'll gag you again, understand?"

Buck nodded. He heard Chedan move toward him and felt fingers on the bandanna knot. When the gag was removed, he let his head fall back to the ground. Sand was gritty against his scalp as it worked through hair not quite a quarter inch long. It stuck to the beard of equal length when he said in a soft, shaking voice: "I had just been promoted to full marshal when Pete Roy robbed the mail coach. Roy eluded the sheriff and the posse, and headed north. I . . . tracked him through the Verde Valley, past Geronimo's cave, up into Sycamore Pass, and on into the cañon. That's . . . real strange country up there."

"Yes," Chedan murmured. "Trails lead in. None lead out."

"We were in there for days. I ran out of food. Had to live off the land. Fish. Hunt animals . . . the four-legged kind to eat . . . as well as the two-legged kind named Pete Roy. I came across a pool surrounded by rocks that looked as though someone had just piled them there. The water was red, the color of blood. I thought I was losin' my mind.

"Three weeks it took me to catch Roy. I think we were both more than a little crazy by then. We were lost . . . and to follow Sycamore Creek down to the Verde River . . . sometimes swimmin' when there was no trail and no other way past the cliffs . . . But I brought him in. God, but he hates me for that.

He swore he'd get me one of these days . . . even though I was only doing my job.

"I brought him in after three weeks, and when I finally got home, my wife and daughter were dead. Of typhoid. Dead. I'd been out doin' my job, you see, while they died . . . and now, my boss calls me disposable and sends the men I thought were my friends out to kill me so the man I am doin' my job by takin' to prison can escape and can lead them to his loot." He laughed faintly. Though his eyes were still tightly shut, a tear escaped and slid down his temple. His voice was so quiet that the Apache could hardly hear him when he finished: "Because my family died while I was out doin' my job, I'm . . . disposable."

"So, what do you plan to do now?"

Again, Buck snorted a brief laugh. "What do I plan to do now? What do I plan to do now. I . . . plan to keep trackin' Gibbs, all the way to the money. Then, I'm goin' to bring him and the money back and throw them both in Lon Humbert's face. Then, you can take Gibbs on back to Yuma and claim your bounty."

"What about Stoner and his partner?"

"I . . . don't know. I'll have to think about that. All I know right now is . . . they'd better not stand between me and gettin' Gibbs to Yuma.

"You can unlock me now, Chedan. I've got myself in hand."

"You sure?"

"Yeah, I'm sure. And . . . thank you." Eyes still closed, Buck sighed heavily before he grinned, saying: "Not often I have the occasion to thank somebody for wallopin' me, but you did the right thing."

The Apache rose, untied Fyffe's ankles, unlocked the manacles, and put the chains and their key in his saddlebags. He turned back to the fire to find his companion sitting with one knee drawn up and his face dropped into the crook of an elbow. When Buck blotted his eyes on his shirtsleeve and looked up, the stubble-hair, four-day growth of beard and expression made him into a haggard old man.

He dusted sand from his head with both hands before he asked: "And you, Chedan? What are you gonna do now?"

Chedan shrugged. "For me, nothin' has changed, except I'm now sure of who you are. You've got my help. But, as I see it, we have two ways to go."

"Let's hear 'em."

"We can keep trailing Gibbs, Stoner, and . . . uh . . ."

"Glover. Felix Glover."

"Yeah, Glover . . . and take the chance of being discovered, or we can head out straight for Jerome by a different trail. This is my country. I know the paths."

Buck thought about that for a hard moment. Finally, he said: "We know they're headed for Jerome. I don't really give a damn what they do between here and there, so long as they get there. But s'pose we cut around them, wait for them up north, and they don't show? I know it's risky to keep tailin' them like this, but I think I'd feel better if I could keep a constant eye on them."

"Your choice." Chedan tilted his head toward Root's corpse. "What you want to do with him?"

Buck heaved to his feet. "Let's bury him, else he draws varmints."

They confiscated Root's money, weapons, horse, and trail supplies before Fyffe put Gil in the ground. Buck had to do most of the burying himself because Chedan muttered that it was bad luck to touch the dead.

They slept the rest of the night and were up at dawn to continue following the trio ahead of them. Fyffe didn't know that only some ten miles to the west, Pete Roy and Joe McNair had come on hard during the day, riding the same road they used because it was the one and only, on horses they had "borrowed" from the citizens of Ehrenberg.

* * * * *

Luther Gibbs was not happy. While he was grateful for the two strangers' company at night, during the day he somehow got the feeling they shared a secret he wasn't in on and were laughing at him. When they'd camped for the night last evening, the one who called himself Jack Stone asked him to tell them about some of his past cases, who he had run down and brought in, how long he'd been a federal marshal, and so on. Drawing on what he recalled that Buck Fyffe had told him, he said he hailed from Virginia and had been a marshal for eleven years, but got around detailing his supposed career activities by saying a government agent didn't disclose case histories.

Mr. Stone had grinned at Mr. Smith and let it ride. Still, Luther felt something wasn't right. It made him edgy and short-tempered to the point that he almost wished he hadn't taken up with them.

Besides, there was something going on out there on his back trail he couldn't fathom. One night, he'd heard what he thought was a man shouting. It sounded to him like someone nearly insane with rage, but it had stopped before he could pinpoint the source, and now he wondered if it wasn't merely his imagination creating voices and words out of the wind in mesquite branches.

A few miles to the west, Joe McNair was equally unhappy. Try as he would, he couldn't erase the sight of Pete Roy coldly and methodically smothering that little boy. Killing a convict and using any means necessary to force a robber to disclose his cache location was one thing. But a little nine- or ten-year-old boy?

And then, there had been the lad's mother there at the dock in Ehrenberg, waiting for her son to get off the paddle-wheeler. The anxious look. The hands clasped to the bosom. She had stopped him and Roy when they reached the land end of the gangplank to ask: "Is there a boy aboard that boat?"

Pete had said smoothly: "Yes, Ma'am, there was, but I think he got off with his Ma and Pa some distance downriver."

"No," the young mother said. "No, I mean a little boy traveling alone with a tag pinned to his shirt. My son has brown hair and brown eyes. In her letter to me, my sister said she would put a tag on Billy. Did you see . . . ?"

"Ma'am," Roy said, "why'nt you go ask the captain?"

"Yes, I'll do that. Thank you for your kindness, sir."

'Thank you for your kindness?' The mother said that to the man who had murdered her son. McNair felt no guilt about how he and Harold Johnson had killed Moses Little, but that boy . . .

He looked at Roy in terror, and when Pete pointed out two good-looking horses in a nearby corral with no one in attendance and said, "I like those," he'd been too fainthearted to hang back. He thought that in less than a week, he had gone from being a respected Yuma Territorial Prison guard to—he guessed he could say—an accessory to two killings, and now a horse thief. One thing seemed to lead to another. How much lower could he go? So far, he hadn't raped a woman or eaten worms, but the way things proceeded here, those events didn't seem too far in the offing!

There had been a tentative effort by townspeople hastily organized into a posse that rode a short way out into the desert in search of the horses. Roy and McNair lost some time hiding in an arroyo until the group passed, then passed again on their return to Ehrenberg, but Joe was gratified that he wasn't going to be hung as a horse thief. At least, not today.

The scratch in the desert that might be called a road now passed through stands of saguaro, a bristling cholla forest so thick that travelers in all three groups had to keep to the cleared path in defense of their horses and legs, then onward to an ever-rising landscape. Once, they all had to stand aside to let the stagecoach from Ehrenberg to Prescott thunder past. Another day, after they hit the Woolsey Trail that was beginning to be called the Black Cañon Road, a different coach, this one with Arizona Stage Company emblazoned on its doors, passed them headed south on the overnight trip from Prescott to the dusty little desert town of Phoenix.

Fyffe and Chedan rode without speaking for the most part, largely because Fyffe was now a grimly quiet man. The Apache watched his Indah companion closely, and became almost as wary of him as McNair was of Roy.

Buck's face was hidden by an inch-long beard and mustache shades darker than the slower growing, light-brown hair. Specks of white grizzled the whiskers and added years to Fyffe's apparent age.

The narrow blue eyes were cold and deep, as though whatever thoughts the mind behind them held lay like a hidden high mountain winter pool whose very quiet kept it from freezing until one dipped a finger into it, and the disturbed water flashed into solid ice. He sat the saddle astride his big black mule and led Gilbert Root's horse. His hat was pulled low over his eyes, his clothing trail dusty and reeking of sweat. He merely followed Luther Gibbs, Josh Stoner, and Felix Glover silently and relentlessly, for he was a man used and betrayed by his own and all thoughts ran toward revenge.

The days passed relatively uneventfully for Fyffe and Chedan until Pete Roy and Joe McNair caught up with them

CHAPTER ELEVEN

"Riders comin'," Buck said succinctly.

Chedan nodded but didn't look back. "I know it. They been gettin' closer the last couple of days. What do you want to do about them?"

"Nothin'. Let 'em pass on. We can't confront someone merely because they're usin' the same road. Still, when they're down in one of those dips back there, let's just step out into the brush here and let 'em go. If they've seen us, they may think we're just heat visions or the like."

Chedan's green eyes went wide in appreciation. "Hau! You think like an Apache, Buck." He flashed a look over his shoulder at their back trail. "And . . . now."

Immediately, Fyffe reined Barbarossa off the road and pulled Root's gelding with him. Chedan slid from his pony's back. He slapped the dun after Buck, eased into the brush, and broke a tamarisk branch. Watching the western road carefully, he timed it so the oncoming riders would be down in the next dip before he leaped back out into the path and swept away tracks as he retreated into hiding.

Buck caught the Indian's pony. He dismounted and held Barbarossa and the horses until Chedan joined him; then they stood motionlessly side-by-side behind the tamarisk to wait for the strangers.

The two on-comers did pass, but at a slow trot, their fingers at their sidearms and eyes searching the landscape on both sides of the road. They had obviously seen riders ahead of them who appeared to have vanished, and wondered where they had gone. Their reduced pace let both Buck and Chedan get a good look at them, and Fyffe sank teeth into his lower lip to keep from cursing out loud.

Buck didn't know one of the men, but if that other—the one dressed in gray pants, his undershirt because he'd taken off his jacket and shirt, no hat but his head shielded from the sun with a blue bandanna bound like a Gypsy's over his skull—was who he thought he was . . .

When the riders passed onward, Chedan muttered: "I don't know who the one on the pinto is, but if I'm right, that other one is Joe McNair. He is a guard from Yuma prison."

Buck darted a sharp glance at him. "You sure?"

"Not really, but I think so. I been workin' for the prison since it opened on July 1st last year. Been with them almost exactly a year and got to know most all the guards pretty well. I think that's Joe McNair. But that other hombre . . ." He shook his head. "He looks familiar to me, though I can't place him. Not a guard, but . . ."

"Would you call him an inmate? Say . . . Pete Roy?"

Chedan's green eyes narrowed thoughtfully. "The one always in trouble? Been dragging a ball and chain around most of his stay? Uh . . . yeah. Possibly."

"Shit," Buck breathed. "How the flamin' hel . . .?" Slowly, he sank to sit on his heels, his expression grimly closed. "I thought it was Pete, but . . . my gawd, this is some kettle of crawdads, ain't it!"

"What? Why?" Chedan also squatted on the sand, his elbows on his knees, the broken branch still in his hands.

Buck slid a glance up the road. "Look what we got here, now. Luther Gibbs is headin' beyond the Verde Valley to get his loot. Josh Stoner and Felix Glover are ridin' with him to keep an eye on him and also retrieve Southwestern's money. Now comes Pete Roy, no doubt after my hide—he hates my innards enough to kill a dozen men to get at me—along with some Yuma guard. How the hell Pete got out of prison, I don't know, but there he is. Prob'ly that guard helped him, but why . . . unless—" He swung around to flash an astonished look at Chedan. "Unless Moses Little told them the actual hiding place! You don't s'pose Moses told those two about the money and where Luther hid it, do you?"

"I wouldn't know," the Apache murmured. "Maybe . . . Aw, hell, I wouldn't know."

"Speakin' of knowin' . . . Gibbs, Stoner, Glover, and Roy all know me. That guard . . ."

"McNair. Joe McNair."

"Yeah. McNair prob'ly knows you by sight. If they all join up . . ."

Silence held between them for a long moment before Buck abruptly looked again at the Apache. "My main objective is to get the money back and put Luther Gibbs in jail where he belongs. That hasn't changed. Stoner, Glover, and McNair are flies in the soup. Still, I can work around them if I have to. But Pete Roy . . ." He shook his head. "Pete's another matter. I said they all know me by sight, but that might not be true. Ol' Gil Root didn't until I told him who I was."

"Buck . . ."

"No, listen . . . listen! Look at me. I think men don't see what they don't expect to see. Stoner, Gibbs, and Glover all think I'm still in Yuma breakin' rocks and eatin' cockroaches . . ."

"But McNair knows you're out. He was among the guards when Lear called me into the turnkey's office. And if he does, so does Roy."

"Yeah. Yeah, that's true. But, Chedan, do I look like Buck Fyffe to you? If I came ridin' in after dark to join up with that pack of coyotes, put on a . . . say, a Southern accent, slouch a bit and all, would you know me?"

"Yes." Chedan nodded. "If you're thinking of doing what I think you're thinking of doing, that's suicide, Buck. You'll shoot the whole deal."

Buck leaned closer to the Apache. "Look, McNair knows I'm out of Yuma, yeah, but he also knows you're with me, and he knows your reputation. He would never expect me to be alone. One of these days, Josh and Felix are gonna wonder whatever happened to Gil Root and maybe come lookin' for him. Then what?" He took off his hat and brushed a palm back and forth over what hair had grown out. "Look at me. What do you think?"

Chedan studied the hair that had settled into a skull-hugging cap, the eyes, the beard and mustache, and shook his head. "Well, with the gray in your beard, you do look a lot older than when I first saw you, but what has that got to do with Root?"

"Gray in my beard? I have gray in my beard?"

"Yeah. Lots. Don't grin like that. When you smile, you look like a kid again. But, Buck, even if you successfully join up with them, what's your purpose? What do you think to gain by it? And what is it about Root?"

"I'm gonna make good use of Gil's disappearance. Look, Chedan, we got five men there, each and every one of 'em a man-hunter and killer or owlhoot. Josh Stoner is one who brings 'em back dead rather than alive. Felix Glover is about the fastest gun you've ever seen. Ol' Luther, well, he's Luther. I don't know about that Yuma guard, but Pete Roy, he's enough to scare the piss right out of a loco bear.

"Now, here we have you and me. You can't go in because both Roy and McNair would know you right off . . . how many Injuns have eyes the color of yours? But I figger they would never imagine that I . . . me . . . Buck Fyffe . . . would walk right into their camp and say . . . 'Howdy, boys.' Maybe ridin' with them is safer in the long run than continuing to track them, especially when we hit the Hill where there's no cover and only one road up the escarpment.

"Even if you back me up, I don't think just you and I can handle that bunch unless we ambush them, and we're not murderers. I think the only way we got to go is to divide and conquer. Take 'em out one-by-one with damned good excuses should any of the rest ask, until there's no one left but ol' Luther and his cache.

"Can you keep up with us . . . you ridin' in the brush instead of on the road?"

"*No hay problema.* But Buck are you that good a gunhand?"

"I'm gonna have to be, ain't I?"

Chedan sighed heavily. "I think you're sun-mad. It's never going to work. What are you going to do if they all recognize you at once?"

"Duck," Fyffe said shortly. He rose and began transferring saddlebags and his bedroll from Barbarossa to Root's horse.

When he tied his own saddle on behind Gil's, Chedan said a string of words in his own language that by their tone told Buck the Apache was maligning his ancestry and intelligence before the mutter ended. "All right, so you're going to do it. What are you going to call yourself should I need to know your name?"

Buck paused a moment, considering that. He thought about the names he and Laurie had come up with prior to Phoebe's birth. Had the baby been a boy, they had settled on Martin Allen Fyffe. They would have named the next child that had Laurie lived long enough to bear him a son. Allen could also be used as a surname. He said it.

"Martin Allen," Chedan repeated, memorizing the Indah label. "Got it."

* * * * *

"Hold on, men!" Under Pete Roy's orders, Joe McNair called after the three riding the road ahead and kicked his weary mount into a faster pace. Roy followed closely.

Gibbs, Stoner, and Glover reined in and turned to scowl at the strangers. Gibbs and Stoner let hands drift toward gun butts. Glover slid his shoulder weapon from its scabbard and turned his horse sideways so the barrel lying across his thighs pointed at the newcomers.

McNair halted his mount a respectful distance away and said: "My name's . . . uh . . . Joe Smith. This is my partner, P-Pete . . . Jones. We're guards from Yuma Territorial Prison lookin' for an escapee. You seen a white man ridin' with an Injun lately?"

The bits and pieces of guard's uniform both McNair and Roy still wore, including the kepi-style cap on Joe's head, lent credence to "Smith's" claim of employment. Still, Josh Stoner snapped: "I thought Yuma hired Apaches for that job."

Pete said quickly: "Usually do, but we had a break recently. All our Injun trackers headed south into the Gila Valley or on down to Mexico lookin' there, so we come this way. You seen two other riders?"

"Not since we left Ehrenberg a week ago," Josh said. "Who you lookin' for?"

"You prob'ly never heard of 'im. Wel . . ."

"Maybe I wouldn't . . ." Stoner grinned. ". . . but he might have." He inclined his head toward Luther. "That there is US Marshal Buck Fyffe. Maybe he's heard of your man."

"Oh, yeah?" Roy went slit-eyed and tense. He stared at the man on the dark bay and studied him closely for a long minute before he scowled. "Well, then, yeah, maybe he has heard of Luther Gibbs."

Luther said quickly: "I know Gibbs. It was me brung him into Yuma a couple of weeks ago. He escaped?"

"Went over the wall." Pete nodded. He slid a cold look at the other two men.

Josh Stoner had a hard time keeping a straight face. He asked of Luther: "What'd you take this Gibbs in for, Marshal Fyffe?"

"What do you care?" Luther snapped.

"Well," Josh said smoothly, "if t'was for leerin' at a lady, that's one thing. We got some rampagin' killer on the loose, that's 'nother. Have to keep a close eye out . . . we got a real hardcase headin' this way. Uh . . . what was he in for?"

"Grand larceny," Luther snarled. To Pete and Joe, he said: "Ain't seen him."

"Grand larceny," Stoner mused, his brown eyes twinkling. "How much is grand?"

Luther slid a look from "Jack Stone" to "Felix Smith," and saw both of them once again appearing to laugh up their shirt-sleeves at him. But he only said: "A lot."

"Oh, well, then, I expect you'll want to be off with these gents lookin' to recapture your man, right?" Josh asked.

"Wrong," Luther growled. "I hauled him in, my job's done. Ain't my fault they can't keep 'im." He glanced down the empty road toward the sinking sun. "Been a long day. Tomorrow, we hit the Hill into the uplands. I'm gonna settle in for the night. You boys stayin' or goin' on?"

"Oh, we'll lite," Josh told him. "A couple more miles on today is useless. Like you once said, Marshal Fyffe, there's safety in numbers."

Joe McNair was looking at Pete Roy in puzzled fear. He'd heard about Buck Fyffe over and over since he and Roy had met on the Colonel Stanton. Here was one called by that name, and the hatred Roy expressed had led him to believe that Pete would kill Fyffe on sight. Yet there he sat astride the pinto, doing nothing but scowling at the marshal. True, the man called Buck Fyffe didn't look a whole lot like the hairless, beardless, desperate man he'd seen in Yuma, but maybe . . .

Still, Roy stared and did nothing, said nothing until the talkative hombre on the roan mare asked: "You boys beddin' down with us or movin' on tonight?"

Roy said softly: "Can't hunt a man in the dark. I see no reason not to halt, 'specially since we got Federal Marshal Fyffe here to look out for our persons. Thank you kindly for your invite. Yeah, we'll stay."

As they turned their horses off the road toward a group of building-sized beige rocks casting shadows across the land, Felix urged his mount up beside Josh to whisper: "I don't like this. We got too many Smiths and Joneses here, and that one who calls himself Joe Smith looks so damned scared of that so-called Jones, he like to passes out every time Jones looks at him."

"I know it," Stoner murmured.

"And Buck escaped Yuma? My gawd, if Buck's out of Yuma, he's gonna come lookin' for Luther, ain't he? Then what?"

"That don't mean anything to us, except that we got to protect Gibbs from him until after we get the money. Fyffe don't know we had any part in his bein' put away. He ain't after us. Besides, don't forget that we got Gil tight on our back trail, keepin' a good eye on us. Any trouble arises, he'll help out."

"Boy, I don't like this a'tall."

"Nor do I, amigo. But just keep thinkin' about that big pot at the end of our rainbow."

Felix heaved a sigh and followed Stoner following Luther Gibbs toward their night shelter. Joe and Pete brought up the rear.

They finished a tense dinner of guarded conversation full of dangerous undercurrents and were settled back, smoking and drinking coffee, when a voice called out of the desert darkness: "Hey, y'all, doan yew shoot me, now! Ah'm comin' in harmless, heah, with mah hands high! Doan yew shoot, gents! All Ah want is some company foah the night!"

CHAPTER TWELVE

Fyffe sat motionlessly astride Gilbert Root's gelding and not only kept both hands in the air but held his breath when five pistols became aimed in his direction. Josh Stoner snapped: "Come into the firelight so we can see you, hombre, but take it slow and easy, else you're dead!"

Buck continued his heavy Southern accent. "Yussuh, Ah'll dew that. Yessuh, doan shoot! An' afore yew ask, suh, Ah didn't steal this heah hoss. He hain't mine, Ah'll grant yew that, but Ah sho didn' steal 'im." He squeezed thighs against the gelding's ribs to urge the animal forward.

Firelight showed a travel-filthy man dressed in a black vest and pants over a shirt that might once have been white, but all were dust-covered into nearly one color. The black hat was pulled so low over the eyebrows there wasn't much to be seen of the face but a sunburned nose above a gray-shot beard.

"Who are you?" Stoner asked.

"Mah name's Martin Allen . . . outta Mobile, Alabamy. Ah got kinfolk livin' in a place called Dewey neah some place called Prescott. Come to live with them. But, hell, y'all got bunches of nothin' out heah. Ah missed mah way an' ended up at some big rivah out yondah. Hain't seen no rivah that size since the Mississippi or Missoura. Folks in some town theah hadda good laugh on me afore they pointed me this way, so . . ." He shrugged.

Felix murmured to Josh: "That's Gil's horse he's riding."

"I know it," Stoner agreed grimly, but before he could ask, Luther posed the question.

"You said that ain't yore animal?"

"No suh, it hain't. Mah pore ol' mare, she got herse'f such a shin splint, Ah had to let 'er go. Ah was walkin' yondah carryin' mah saddle an' bedroll, when Ah come across this heah hoss all geared lahk he belonged to somebody, but theah warn't nobody aroun' Ah could see. Ah hain't nevah been one to leave nobody in the same fix Ah was in, so Ah caught this heah beast an' went lookin' foah the ownah. Can Ah please put mah hands daown, gents? Mah arms is gittin' tahrd."

"All right, step down, but be careful how you do it," Stoner growled.

Buck nodded and eased out of the saddle. So far, neither Pete Roy nor the Yuma guard who Chedan said was named Joe McNair had said anything, just merely stared suspiciously at him. He led the horse a little closer to the fire, but not too near. Holding reins in both hands, he squatted on his heels, then used one hand to flip his hat brim up flat in front, but didn't remove the hat itself. It was a calculated risk; he almost dared the men to recognize him.

"And did you locate the horse's owner?" Felix asked.

"Yessuh, Ah believe so. Leastways, Ah foun' a gent layed out behind a bush with his throat cut."

"Throat cut!" Josh leaned forward, scowling. "How long ago was this?"

"Some three or moah days ago. Somebody practically chopped the po' boy's haid off." Buck watched Stoner and Glover slide looks at each other before he went on. "Ah give the gent a propah buryin'. Said a prayah ovah him lahk mah mama done taught me. Put 'im in as deep a hole as Ah could manage . . . least Ah could do fo' the use of his hoss an' all."

Felix snapped: "Did you see anyone else around? Anyone who . . ."

"No, suh. Hain't seen nobody but yew gents since Ah left that theah li'l town at the rivah . . . 'cept once, Ah neah got run daown by a stagecoach. Shit, Ah'dda knowed theah was a stage goin' this-away, Ah'dda took it 'stead of goin' it alone, but . . . no suh, hain't been no Injuns, no otha travelers 'cept yew, an' since y'all are movin' on togethah, 'lessen y'all done the po' gent in, it's a pure mystery to me who cut his throat. Mind if Ah have some of yoah coffee, gents?"

Buck was rewarded by hard looks darted from Josh and Felix toward Pete and Joe. He let the suspicion fester for a moment—he could see the knowledge that no strangers other than himself, Roy, and McNair, had either approached or passed recently, raising the question in Marshal Stoner's and Felix Glover's minds of who, exactly, had killed Gil Root. Luther obviously hadn't known about Gil; his expression held casual interest and that was all.

Atop the rocks, from the niche where he silently settled in for the night, Chedan watched, listened, and grinned to himself. He could see Buck's "divide-and-conquer" plan getting off to a good start.

What surprised both Buck and Chedan was that it was neither Josh nor Felix who took the bait, but Joe McNair.

* * * * *

Buck got very little sleep that night. He watched everyone watching everyone else, including him, and thought: *I said it right when I called these men a pack of coyotes. Worst lot I've had the misfortune of meeting-up with . . . outside of Yuma Prison, that is.*

Of course, introductions had been performed, with everybody giving assumed names. He'd nodded to each man in turn, recalled Chedan's comment that his smile made him look like a kid, kept it serious and solemn, and noted that when Luther Gibbs was called Marshal Buck Fyffe, Pete Roy's expression almost became a leer. So did Stoner's and Glover's. They all knew Gibbs wasn't him, but they went along with it! Why?

Feeling that things were growing stranger by the minute, Buck lay his bedroll out between the fire and the road to give himself an open avenue of escape should the need arise, and pretended to sleep, but continued to watch the others through his eyelashes. Surprisingly, Roy's attention seemed focused more on Joe McNair than on the others. Again, why? What was Pete afraid Joe would do or say that might cause a problem?

And that McNair was terrified of Roy would have been obvious to a blind man! Once, McNair rose silently from his bedroll, but Roy propped himself up on an elbow and hissed: "Where ya goin', Joe?"

McNair froze in the act of reaching for his blanket. He choked out: "J-Just to take a leak, Pete. That's all."

"Good idea." Roy grinned. "I'll come with you."

Buck noted that Pete wore his gun belt to bed and that his palm rested on the pistol butt while he followed McNair into the darkness. He hoped Joe could work up some pee out there, else he was probably in worse trouble.

Both returned shortly, and nothing else happened. Not until after breakfast was over and the group saddled up did matters take a turn.

Luther headed for the brush "to do his business." As Roy had said during the darkness, McNair commented, "Good idea," and followed. Buck put on a slouched shuffle, like a farmer plodding behind a plow, and also headed in that direction, but his brows rose up under his hat when he saw that for once, Pete didn't seem to notice Joe leave.

Luther had his pants down around his ankles and his bare buttocks an inch above the sand when McNair stepped up beside him and opened his own pants, but hissed: "Marshal, I gotta talk to you, urgent!"

Buck selected a bush a few paces aside, far enough away that he hoped he wouldn't be noticed but close enough to hear what went on between Luther and Joe. He relieved himself quickly and put himself back together while Gibbs scowled up at McNair and snapped: "Good gawd, can't a man even do his business in peace without . . ."

Joe burst out in one continuous, breathless whisper, an odd mix of truth and lie: "Marsha . . . Marshal, I was off duty when you got brought in as Luther Gibbs, but I was there when the superintendent let you go . . . and surely you know that hombre out there who says he's Pete Jones ain't Pete Jones . . . he's Pete Roy, a convict escaped from Yuma . . . 'cause he knows you, I believe! Pete forced me and Harold Johnson to help him escape, then he kilt Harold and then a little boy on the paddle-wheeler, then he cut that hombre's throat back there and now he's gunnin' fer you . . . I don't know why he ain't come after you yet, but you know he will, and you gotta help me, Marshal, or we're both dead!"

Luther still squatted, staring up at him with his mouth open and buttocks shining in the strengthening morning light. He turned red, birthed a turd, finished, stood, pulled up his pants, and sucked teeth for a moment before he growled: "Pete ain't gonna gun me. You said it yourself . . . he was gonna do it, he'd have tried before now. Take care of yore own problems, and leave me outta it!"

Joe looked stunned. He gasped: "But you're a marshal! I tol' you that bastard escaped Yuma . . . killed guards . . . strangled a helpless li'l boy 'cause the child was witness to one murder . . . cut that pilgrim's throat back there just for fun! It's your job to take hard cases like that in! You . . ."

"I got business up north. You want Pete back in Yuma, take 'im yourself. You're packin' iron, use it!" Luther turned away.

Joe grabbed his arm to stop him. He whispered: "Marshal Fyffe, I can make it worth your while! I happen to know where there's a heap of cash just waitin' on who gits to it first! You help me, and I'll let you in on . . ."

"Hey! You boys gonna take all day? We're ready to go!" Stoner's voice cut McNair off.

Buck hurriedly made his way around the roadside of the rocks and back into camp. He remembered to slouch and shuffle when he came into sight, and kept his hat pulled low over his eyes. He damned Josh's interruption of Joe's plea to Luther, because it seemed he'd been about to hear something important, something about a "heap of cash"—undoubtedly Southwestern's stolen money.

He discovered Stoner examining the .44-40 Winchester stuck in the scabbard of the extra saddle tied to the back of Gil Root's gear. The dead Southwestern security man's own weapon was in the other scabbard. He made a pretense of brushing twigs off his pants legs and tying the thigh strings to settle his holster to keep his head down, because passing as someone else in the firelighted dark was one thing, while closeup in the daylight was something else.

Stoner said: "Fine weapon. Looks new. Ain't this what the guards down at Yuma Prison usually carry?"

Buck sidled past Josh to check his saddle cinch. He kept his back to the man while he said: "Ah wouldn' know, suh. Lahk this hoss, them rifles hain't mine, neithah." He thought quickly to devise an explanation and continue his "divide-and-conquer" plan as he swung astride and looked down at Stoner. "Ah come heah with only ol' Trudy on me." He patted the scarred pistol grip. "This heah weapon come with the saddle." He indicated Root's rifle. "But Ah foun' that Winchestah layin' neah the bushes by that po' throat-cut gent Ah buried. Looked lahk somebody done fo'got it. Been a crime to jus' let it lay. But Mistuh Jones ovah theah," he nodded at Pete Roy, "he's got one jus' lahk it . . . maybe yew best ask him."

Stoner turned to scowl at "Jones." When Pete sauntered over to examine the rifle, Buck lifted a hand to scratch at beard and mustache, effectively hiding most of his face.

Roy took the weapon, looked it over, and handed it back to Buck. He said shortly: "Yep, is like the weapons Yuma guards use. So what? They the only ones got .44-40s aroun' here?"

Buck slid a look at Joe McNair, now back in the clearing. He said to Roy: "Yew carryin' a Winchestah. Yew one of them Yuma guards?"

"Am," Pete scowled. "So?"

Buck indicated McNair. "He a Yuma guard?"

Roy turned to look at Joe. "Yeah. So?"

"How come he hain't carryin' no .44-40? He lose his?"

Everyone except Luther turned to scowl at McNair. Joe didn't know what was going on. He saw the men staring at him and frowned back. "What . . . I take too long easin' my innards or somethin'?"

Stoner asked: "Why ain't you totin' a rifle, Mr. . . . Smith?"

McNair flashed a quick look at Roy before he answered: "I h-had one, but I . . . lost it in the river on the way here."

"He did that." Pete nodded. "I seen it."

"So, you came upriver by steamer instead of ridin' from Yuma?"

"Yeah!" Roy snapped. "So what? What is this, anyway?"

"Seems to me," Josh mused, "that if you was huntin' a convict escaped from prison like you claim, you'd have tracked him all the way. How d'you intend to locate his trail up here without you knowin' which way he went?"

Roy's eyes went slitted and even hotter than usual. He let his hand drift toward his sidearm. "We got our ways," he snarled to Stoner. "How much you know 'bout trackin' a man, anyhow?"

Everyone in camp tensed. Felix's fingers grazed his pistol grip. Luther took a few steps back, well away from the line of fire. McNair's eyes widened briefly before he also moved aside. Astride Root's horse, Buck waited to see what would happen.

Josh didn't go for his gun. He merely lifted a brow speculatively at Pete, sent a significant look at the others, and turned his back on Roy to walk toward his own mount.

You wouldn't have done that if you knew who you were dealing with, Josh, Buck thought grimly.

Eyes still fixed on Stoner, Roy hesitated before he dropped his hand and stumped toward his own animal.

Buck slid the .44-40 into the extra scabbard and asked: "Yew gents mind if Ah tag along aftah y'all a while? We all seem to be goin' the same way, and since Ah'm a strangah in this heah country, it'd sho be a comfo't to me."

No one agreed or objected. Taking silence as tacit permission, when the group mounted and moved out, he followed. He didn't mind eating their dust; he wanted to stay close enough to be with them, but far enough back to keep his anonymity intact.

He cast a quick look around once, searching for sign of Chedan, but didn't see him. That meant nothing. He figured the Apache was out there, and he knew that if Chedan didn't want to be seen, he wouldn't be, and concentrated on what he'd heard pass between Joe McNair and Luther.

Unless there was some heap of cash lying around out there, other than Southwestern's, that he hadn't heard about, it had to be Gibbs's loot. So if it was Southwestern's money, how would McNair know about it, unless Moses Little had told him? And why, when McNair was so obviously terrified of Pete Roy, did the Yuma guard stay with the owlhoot, unless they had the same goal in mind? Or why didn't Pete just stick a knife into Joe in the dark of some night or vice versa?

The only reason seemed to be that each knew something the other didn't . . . like where that heap of cash was actually hidden, or what he himself looked like. Was that it? Pete knew him, yeah, but then, McNair thought Luther was him. Besides, why should McNair care about him at all? And if Moses Little had told Joe McNair about the money, why had Joe helped Pete Roy escape and not Little?

Strange!

Finally, if Luther ever came to the same conclusion he had— that McNair knew where to find Southwestern's twenty-five thousand, Pete Roy be damned—Joe McNair was a dead man.

Well, no way was Luther going to disclose the location of his cache. That meant that if he himself was going to find it, he had to get directions from Joe or see that Gibbs lived long enough to lead him to it. That almost made him into Luther's and McNair's bodyguard, didn't it!

Shit!

Morosely, he rode onward.

CHAPTER THIRTEEN

Because Fyffe was supposed to be a stranger in this area who didn't know the way and obviously couldn't lead, he had a legitimate excuse to bring up the rear and was left out of things. His position as follower also gave him a good view of what went on among the others.

Stoner and Glover didn't want Pete Roy and Joe McNair behind them. Roy wanted the Yuma guard up front where he could keep an eye and ear on the man. Had the situation not been so dangerous, Buck would have laughed while he watched his companions jockeying for position on the road.

He was surprised that he hadn't fallen under suspicion for Gil Root's death, but it seemed his innocent plowboy act was effective enough to put him out of contention as a likely candidate for murderer of the day. Still, he took every opportunity to cautiously advance his "divide-and-conquer" strategy.

They labored up Antelope Hill on the winding, steep, narrow, switchback trail between the tiny islands of population named Bumble Bee and Cordes to the north, with Mayer, Humboldt, and Dewey not too many miles ahead. When the sun plunged below the rugged forested mountaintops, they stopped for the night by a swift-running creek in the shadows of tall rocks and taller Ponderosa pine.

Getting no help from Luther Gibbs, who Joe McNair thought was Marshal Buck Fyffe, when Pete Roy's back was turned, Joe found an opportunity to approach Felix Glover. After a sparse dinner everyone contributed supplies to, Buck watched Felix go to the creek to wash out a tin coffee cup. McNair walked up and knelt beside Glover. On hands and knees, Joe appeared to lean close to the rippled water to drink, but in fact, murmured to Felix: "You interested in a real big payroll, boy?"

Glover slid a surprised look at him. "Uh . . . yeah, I could use a few dollars. How much are we talkin' about?"

"Lots. More'n you ever seen before in yore life."

"Well, ain't you sharin' it with yore pardner, Mr. Jones, over there?"

McNair leaned to again lower his face near the creek surface and pretended to drink, but instead whispered: "Jones ain't Jones, he's an escaped convict from Yuma named Pete Roy. He's the one what cut that hombre's throat on our back trail, and you want half of twenty-five thousand dollars, you kill him for me and the money's yours."

"Why don't you do the job yourself? Then the whole count would be yours."

"'Cause he watches me all the time. I seen him kill! He enjoys it, and if I tried it and din't do the job complete first off, my gawd, you don't know what he'd do to me! I need help, man! Will you . . ."

Fyffe saw the whole thing but couldn't hear what was said. He did hear Roy growl from across the camp: "Smith! You gonna drink the crick dry? Git over here! We gotta figger out what we're gonna do to find our man when we hit Prescott tomorrow or the next day!"

"Yeah, yeah," McNair answered. As he rose to return to the fire, he hissed to Glover: "Give it some thought."

Buck stood and took the tin cup and plate he'd found in Gil Root's saddlebags to the stream to also wash them. While he was there, and as long as his back was to the others, he took off his hat, dunked his head, and scrubbed both his beard and what hair he had with cool water, for all were stiffly fouled with sweat and trail dust. He wiped hands hard over his scalp and was just reaching for his hat when bushes shivered on the other side of the creek. Startled, he looked up to see Chedan—merely a face barely outlined among the leaves and nothing else—looking back at him.

The Apache murmured: "There's a band of Chiricahua up ahead, Martin Allen. I had a talk with them. Geronimo ain't with them."

Buck whispered: "What are Bedonkohe Apaches doin' this far north and west? They on the warpath again?"

"No. They've got a medicine man leading them. They're headed up north to get blue stones and paint-rock for coloring pottery and making body paint. They're peaceful right now, but that doesn't mean they won't take the time to rid our lands of a few white men, come the opportunity. I'll watch out."

Buck blinked, and in that moment, Chedan was gone. Thinking: *Shit, just what I need . . . a bunch of Indians to complicate things!,* he jammed his hat over his wet hair, picked up his plate and cup, and returned to the fire in time to see Glover whispering into Stoner's ear, McNair looking tense and miserable beside Roy, and Luther Gibbs lounging over his unfinished coffee while he picked at his teeth with a pine needle.

Once again, he thought: *What a pack of varmints!* Abruptly, he caught Pete grinning at him. He stored his eating utensils, then eased down against a boulder across the fire from Roy, loosened his six-shooter in its holster, and pulled his hat brim low over his eyes before he noted: "Yew look lahk yew got somethin' to say to me, Mistuh Jones. Why'nt yew jus' go ahaid an' spit it out?"

Pete lifted his cup. For all that his eyes were hard and cold over the rim as he sipped coffee, they burned to some private humor. He said: "I was just recollectin' a occurrence in my past, Mr. . . . Allen . . . before I started to work for the prison. Once . . . oh, a year or so ago . . . me and another fellah was up in the Verde Valley north of here. One of us was a lawman, and one of us was a fugitive, one of us chasin' t'other, as it were.

"Well, we ended up in Sycamore Cañon, and that place is haunted, y'know? Bad things happen to jus' about ever'body that goes in there."

"Dew tell," Buck murmured, but tensed, suddenly feeling cold. Had Pete finally recognized him?

"Well, we got lost in there, and as it turned out, we ended up havin' to work t'gether, him and me. The law and the lawless, you might say, workin' t'gether jus' to survive. I mean, you'd think an experience like that would change a man inside, as well as out, y'know? The lawless considered that since he helped the lawman live, maybe the lawman would jus' natural look t'other way when they got outta there in gratitude, or out of built-up comradeship, or the like. But no. The lawman figgered the law as the law, y'know? He sent the lawless off to jail. His insides wasn't changed at all.

"But then, his outsides was. Oh, yes, his outsides surely was. That lawman started out neat and clean and close-shaved, but in his struggle to survive . . ." Roy's tone grew more sarcastic with each word, the glitter in his eyes hotter and harder. ". . .

the lawman grew a beard and got ragged and dirty, starved and footsore, and ended up lookin' about like . . ."

An arrow sang through the air and buried itself in Joe McNair's heart. Instantly, all the other men around the campfire, including Buck, grabbed hoglegs and shoulder weapons, scrambled behind any likely shelter, and glared into the darkness beyond the rocks. Faintly, a voice shouted a long string of Athapascan words that ended in a laugh fading as the attacker retreated.

Luther, his expression part fear, part rage, shot indiscriminately at anything that moved out there—a twig, a leaf, a passing bat— until Josh Stoner snarled: "Stop that, man! We can't hear with you blastin' away like an idjit!"

In the following quiet, Buck listened into the night along with everyone else. Unless all Indians sounded alike, that had been Chedan's voice, he knew it, and though he didn't understand most of the words, he did recognize one—Indah—because it was so close to what the Anglos called the Apaches. Indah: white man. Apache: Indian. He had expected to have to protect Joe McNair from Pete or Luther, but sure not from Chedan.

A long, tense, watchful silence ensued. The group had just begun to relax when another arrow took Felix Glover through the left eye. Flint and wood embedded in his brain, he fired his pistol once even as he lurched against the boulder behind him, before nerves shut down and he plunged sideways to lay wedged between two rocks.

Again, Luther peppered the darkness with bullets. This time, Josh and Pete joined him. And again, a laugh faded into the distance.

What Chedan had once said to him, that the reason he ran escapees down for the prison was because it was the only job he knew of where an Apache got paid by whites to kill other white men, popped into Buck's head. What was that devil going to do, sit out there and pick them off one by one? Gil Root had established in the Apache's mind that he, not Luther Gibbs, was in fact Buckley Fyffe, but did Chedan think he was helping him or . . . ?

He glanced at Stoner, Gibbs, and Roy. Now, unless Joe McNair had told Pete, it seemed only Gibbs knew for sure where Southwestern's cash was hidden. While he had planned to divide and thus conquer the others, how the hell did he handle things now? Would Chedan merely pick Roy and Stoner off later on tonight or tomorrow, leaving only him and Luther alive, or had the Apache decided that at fifty dollars a head, he, Luther, Pete, and maybe even McNair's corpse, would bring in one hundred fifty to two hundred dollars, and that was enough to satisfy his needs for a long time?

It seemed that instead of improving, circumstances were growing more iffy by the moment, and whether or not Chedan had been trying to help him, like as not, this night's mayhem wasn't over.

He was now alone with Pete, who wanted revenge, Federal Marshal Josh Stoner who seemed perfectly willing to see him go to prison or die so Luther would betray the location of the cash, and Gibbs who assumed his identity. He felt that both Roy and Stoner knew Luther wasn't him. If Pete had recognized him, how long would it be until he brought Josh in on it, if at al . . . or decided to satisfy that yearning for revenge?

Well, at least the numbers had eased some. It was now only three to one rather than five to one, maybe even three to two, if Chedan was actually trying to help.

Playing his role as a stranger here, he asked: "Y'all thank we should go lookin' foah whoevah t'was kilt them Smith boys, Marshal?"

Both Stoner and Gibbs looked at him, and Buck subdued

a grim smile; in the tension of the situation, Josh had forgotten himself for a moment. He kept his eyes on Luther and didn't acknowledge Stoner, because he wasn't supposed to know that Josh was a lawman.

Gibbs licked lips. He glared around the campsite, scowled out at the dark wilderness surrounding them, listened hard into the night. Finally, he snapped: "No! We can't go runnin' blind through the brush. That's a sure way to end up dead. No, whoever they were, I think they're gone. Besides, regardless of arrows and that string of gibberish, that wasn't no Injun out there. No Injun says anything when he fights you, much less laughs! Uhn-uh. Crazy whites, maybe . . . Injuns, no."

But maybe an Apache schooled by white men? Buck pondered. He said: "Ah hain't too knowledgeable on this sort of thang, gents, but seems to me that first off, we should do somethin' with them daid folks . . . else they draw varmints . . . and second, we gotta set up some kind of look-out heah foah the night. Take turns, and like-a-that." He slid a look at Stoner from under his hat brim, then another at Roy.

Josh nodded. "Yeah. And I'll take first watch."

They confiscated weapons, money, and supplies, moved the corpses to the edge of the campsite, piled what loose rocks they could find over the bodies, and Stoner, in fact, stood first watch. Buck took the second, followed by Pete Roy, and then Luther. Fyffe intended to stay awake to ensure that Roy didn't stick a knife into his heart at the earliest opportunity and also to keep an eye on Gibbs, but pretending slumber betrayed him and became real sleep. When he and Pete awoke at dawn, Stoner and Gibbs were gone. So were all the horses and most of the weapons and food.

"Well, Marshal, ol' friend," Roy grinned softly over the .44-40 he aimed at Buck's heart, "looks like once ag'in, it's jus' you and me, don't it!"

CHAPTER FOURTEEN

Buck froze. His blanket was tangled around his legs. He wore his sidearm, but it was under cloth he would have to throw aside to reach, and though the rifle he'd taken from Gil Root's corpse lay next to him, Pete already held a steady bead on him. To make a play for one weapon or the other at this moment would be suicide.

He held on to what he felt was his own open option. Maybe Roy was sure he was Buck Fyffe, but maybe not . . . It could be mere suspicion on the owlhoot's part.

He cast a quick glance around the campsite before he looked back at Pete and continued his Southern plowboy act. "Foah wha' yew pointin' that theah big ol' shootin' iron at me, Mistuh Jones? And whar'd ever'body go?"

Roy's lip curled in his black-stubbled face. Like Buck's, both his hair and beard were growing out, though his hair seemed to have had a head start on Fyffe's and was longer. His tone a sneer, he said: "Oh, come on, Fyffe, don't try to pull that one on me! I know who you are. Give it up!" The Winchester twitched.

Still prone, and braced by left elbow and right hand, Buck

returned scowl for scowl. "Mistuh Jones, yew feelin' all raht? Marshal Fyffe was that gent bedded daown ovah theah, and it looks lahk him and Mistuh Stone done gone off and lef' us. Yew got eny idea why they done thet? They seemed lahk decent gents to me . . . yew s'pose that theah Injun attack las' night scared 'em off?"

"Buck, cut it out! I know you!" Roy shifted the .44-40 to better his aim.

Buck lifted his right hand in a staying gesture, didn't otherwise move. He said urgently: "Mistuh Jones, yew fahr that theah rifle, and yew'll bring ever' Injun in the territory daown on us! Ah doan know whut yoah problem is, but mah name's Martin Allen, Ah'm up heah from Mobile, Alabamy, come to join kinfolk in Dewey. Ah done made mah way all acrost the land successfu . . . yew hain't gonna shoot me when Ah nevah done yew no wrong and am so close to mah new home, is yew?" He saw the first glimmer of doubt in Pete's eyes and almost held his breath, waiting to see what Roy would do.

Pete snarled: "Take off that hat!"

"Yessuh . . . yessuh . . . sho nuff, Mistuh Jones. Enythin' yew say, suh." Slowly, Buck removed the hat and, holding the brim by finger and thumb, ran the heel of his hand over his skull. His hair was not yet a half-inch long; it lay flat to his scalp. There was no gray in it as there was marking his beard. Sweat had darkened it to almost the same color as his whiskers. He forced himself to meet Roy's eyes openly and kept his expression one of puzzled innocence, but prepared to throw the hat at Pete and simultaneously fling himself aside, though he doubted Roy could miss at this close range.

In the dawn silence that fell over the camp while Pete studied Buck, a few birds greeted the rising sun from high up in the pines around them. This was a different land than the low desert only a few miles below; clear and bright, brushy with mesquite and feathery tamarisk. A few yucca, and great stands of prickly pear bordered forests of Ponderosas tall above shorter, scrubbier Jack pines. Northward, the area further evolved into farming and ranch lands where apples and pears were raised along with cattle.

Finally, Roy smiled grimly. He breathed: "Martin Allen, huh?"

"Yessuh," Buck asserted.

"Out of Mobile, eh?"

Again, Fyffe agreed. "Yessuh. Sho am."

Roy laughed. He twitched the Winchester again. "All right, on your feet, Martin Allen."

Slowly, carefully, Buck settled his hat, snagged the blanket, and unwound it from around his legs.

"Hold it! Take that iron out of leather and set it aside. Be careful how you do it."

"But, suh," Buck began, "should them Injuns attack ag'in . . ."

"If that happens, then you'll have yore weapon back. Git rid of it!"

"Yessuh . . . yessuh . . . doan yew git riled, now, suh." Buck flipped away the trigger guard and pulled the pistol with two fingers. He lay it on the dirt at arm's length. "Now can Ah git up, suh?"

"Easy. Do it easy."

"Yessuh." Buck rose. He stood slouched and seemingly hesitant as he glanced around the campsite and shook his head. It had been mostly cleaned out, except for the saddle he'd used as a pillow, one over where Roy had likewise been bedded down, two canteens, and a couple of saddlebags. He asked: "How long they been gone?"

"Dunno," Pete snapped. "They was gone when I woke up."

He motioned with the rifle. "Gather up that stuff, pick up them two saddles, and let's go."

"Suh!" Buck protested. "Ah hain't no pack brute! Whut yew gonna tote?"

"These here weapons." Roy grinned. With an eye and the rifle close on Buck, he moved to pick Fyffe's .44-40 out of the dirt, slung its strap over his shoulder, retrieved Buck's pistol, stuffed it under his belt, and, still keeping Fyffe covered, walked to the canteens. He hefted them one by one and also passed their straps over his shoulder. "I figger it ain't too far to the next town, and as long as I got a strong back available, I might as well use it. I can always kill you later. Now wrap up them bedrolls and heft everything. I want to get movin'."

Buck stood where he was, trying to find some way out of this. Roy was too far away at the moment to jump, and kept the rifle tight on him. There was nothing close enough to fling himself behind. He couldn't outrun a bullet, and, besides, he recalled up in Sycamore Cañon seeing Pete bring down a quail, taking its head off with one shot. Still trying to delay, he asked: "Hain't we gonna eat somethin' firs', Mistuh Jones? They lef' us a li'l food, and Ah'm hongry."

"We'll eat later. I want to move on in the cool of the mornin'. Now pick that stuff up, I said, so's we can hit the trail, dammit, I ain't gonna tell you ag'in!"

"Yessuh," Buck muttered. "Ah'm doin' it, suh." He turned to roll up his own blanket and lay it beside his saddle and carry-sacks before he went on to do Roy's. He bundled Pete's bedroll, slung it and the saddlebags over his shoulders, picked up Roy's saddle, and returned to his own gear. He remembered to keep his plowboy shuffle, but after he had two bedrolls, the carry-sacks, the saddle blankets, and two saddles on his back, the plod became necessity, for it was a heavy load.

Pete chuckled and jabbed the .44-40 northward. "Move out, Martin Allen."

Mouth grim, Buck again hesitated. He held both saddles over his shoulders with fingers locked under the hollow saddle-bows; he knew he was encumbered and wouldn't be able to move quickly enough to defend himself or overcome Roy, especially since Pete stood some ten feet off. Still, in keeping with his befuddled guise, he began: "Mistuh Jones, suh, Ah cain't . . ."

Roy cut him off. He asked: "Which you want, Mr. Allen? I can blow off a few toes right now, which, I do believe would make walkin' a sight more uncomfortable fer you . . . or I can plug you in the heart, which would put you out of yore misery for good. Or, you can start walkin' up that trail. Lemme know yer choice, now!"

Buck was well enough acquainted with Roy to know he would do any or all of that. Without further protest, he turned toward the road and, once there, headed north. Laughing, Pete followed a few steps behind.

* * * * *

The upgrade was not steep here, but it was steady. The morning was cool; still, laboring under his load made Buck break a sweat. The road was only two ruts centered by sporadic growths of grass and an occasional truncated bush where wheels didn't usually roll, but the tracks were gullied by rain runoff. It was hard, uneven walking, and Fyffe kept to the higher, smoother center so not to turn an ankle in some sharp-sided water trench.

All the while, Roy regaled him with tales of himself and another man lost in Sycamore Cañon, and outlined in vivid detail what he was going to do to that hombre should they ever meet again. Buck made no comment, because he was trying to figure out why Luther hadn't merely taken off alone and why he had chosen Josh rather than himself or Roy to accompany him. Was it because Stoner had said he also was headed for Jerome? He recalled that Josh had indicated that was the case when he first met Gibbs. Was Luther afraid to go it alone what with Indians lurking among the rocks? To the best of his knowledge, Gibbs had never done anything at all by himself, but always ran with a gang to back him up. Or had Stoner been the one to suggest to Gibbs that they leave the others behind?

He resisted the urge to tell Pete that his tales of Sycamore Valley labeled him as the outlaw rather than the lawman, and only listened with half an ear to Roy's descriptions of how long a man could live after being flayed of his hide or how burning his eyes out with a heated pistol barrel made the orbs pop and boil, because something on the ground had caught his attention.

They were now perhaps a mile or mile and a half from the campsite, and he scowled at the grass growing on the middle-of-the-road hump. He walked bent under his burden and with his head down. He had long since seen by their hoofprints that six or seven animals had recently passed, one of them unshod and one whose smaller shoes might indicate a mule. It said to him that Luther and Josh led his and Pete Roy's horses northward, and that it had indeed been Chedan killing men and laughing about it last night, because leading Barbarossa and riding his barefooted pony, the Apache followed Gibbs and Stoner.

And, he noted an odd item. Three tufts of grass stood in the middle of the road, each reared staunchly upright by the knot tied at their middles. It came to him that he'd seen another group knotted just like this a few yards back, but though he'd noticed them, they hadn't made any impression on him at the time.

Scowling, the saddles, blanket rolls, and carry-sacks growing heavier with each step, he now scrutinized the grass he walked over, wondering if this was some sort of sign important to him. A short distance on, he saw another group of three knotted clumps.

Up ahead, the road plunged into a copse of trees and brushy undergrowth. To the right beyond a fringe of pines was nothing but sky-high beige boulders, but to the left, trees almost became forest. Buck was grateful for the shade when—followed more closely by Pete—they entered that stand of trees. There, tied on the hump between wagon ruts, stood a single knotted grass tuft.

This one was different than the others. Its knot bent seed tassels westward toward the thicket clearing urging: *Go that way.*

Buck glanced toward the edge of the road. There was another grass bundle. Its tip also pointed west. Chedan had left him a message as plainly as though he'd written words in the dirt, and though he hadn't been expecting it and hadn't looked for it, the Apache had known how to catch and hold his attention.

Whatever the tracker was trying to tell him, it was obviously important. A short distance on, Fyffe saw another tuft, this one knotted so its tip pointed down the trail, back the way they had come. It said to him that he had passed the place he was to turn off. He needed to go back.

He slid a quick look behind him. Roy still followed at a safe distance, but he was closer. The outlaw almost appeared to be bored, as if herding his plodding prisoner along was becoming a chore. That wasn't good, because when Roy became bored, he found a way to ease it and got even meaner, if that was possible.

Buck chose that moment to stub his toe and sprawl on his face under a tangle of saddles, blankets, saddlebags, and dust. He lay panting for a moment, gathering strength and pinpointing Pete's position in his mind; what he was about to do required every fiber in him to live through it.

"Get up and move along," Pete growled.

The individual parts of Buck's burden slid to each side when he shoved palms against the dirt to lift head and shoulders off the road. He turned partially to look up at Roy and panted: "Suh . . . come on, naow, be reasonable. Yew he'p me a li'l, we'd make a lot bettah time heah. Yew tote yoah geah. Ah tote mine, and . . ."

"I got all I'm gonna carry right now! Up! I ain't got all day, here!"

"Well, then, suh, jus' lemme rest a bit heah, suh, then Ah'l . . ."

"Up, dammit! Pick them supplies up, load yer back, and git movin'!"

"Yessuh . . . yessuh . . ." Buck lurched up onto his knees. Roy was still too far away. He needed Pete closer to make this work. He repositioned the saddlebags over his shoulders and reached for the bedrolls, got one of them across his back, but then more or less collapsed over the second. What he had already picked up fell back to the ground when he turned to sit down on the dirt and pleaded: "Suh . . . please, suh . . . Ah'm done-in." He knew he was pushing it when he finished: "Please let me rest jus' a bit heah, then . . ."

Pete took several steps forward and knocked Buck over when he kicked him hard in the side. He aimed the .44-40. "You got thirty seconds to load up and move out before I start shootin', boy!"

"Aw right . . . gawddammit . . . shit, aw right!" Again, Buck got up, this time to his feet. He draped carry-sacks over his shoulders. Watching Roy out of the corner of his eye, he let the bedrolls lay, reached for one of the saddles, and picked it up by pommel and cantle. He straightened abruptly and swung the heavy wood, leather, and fleece-padded seat at Pete, because he felt that it was escape now, or never.

CHAPTER FIFTEEN

Buck didn't let go of the saddle. The loose girth cinch and straps met the Winchester barrel, flipped around it, wrapped it, and the metal circle at the end of the cinch snagged a protrusion on the .44-40; Fyffe couldn't have done that on purpose had he tried. When he continued his upward swing, the rifle fired, but the bullet whined harmlessly into the treetops as the weapon was jerked out of Roy's grip.

Now Buck opened his hands. Saddle and rifle sailed over his head and plunged to the road behind him as he lunged at Pete. Roy made a grab for his sidearm. He had it drawn but not yet aimed when Buck seized the wrist with both hands and drove his shoulder into Roy's chest.

Though not as tall as Fyffe, Pete was a brute of a man, bulkier and stronger, and Buck knew it. Still, his weight threw Roy backward to the ground. He shoved downward with everything he had, plunged the pistol barrel into the dirt, wrenched his own hogleg from under Pete's belt, and leaped to his feet. Just as he thumbed the hammer and aimed at Roy, Pete jerked his arm up and pressed the trigger on his pistol. Clogged with dirt, the weapon didn't fire.

Pete lurched up onto his knees and grabbed at the second .44-40 whose strap had slid off his shoulder, trying with one hand to get the rifle into position to fire.

Buck set his teeth and squeezed the trigger. The bullet took Pete Roy dead center of the chest but failed to slow him down. Fyffe saw Roy still attempting to raise the Winchester, cocked his pistol, and shot Pete again.

This time, Roy noticed it. Still jockeying the rifle into position with his left hand, he fell over onto his back. Knees drawn up and expression clenched into agonized determination, he struggled to aim the weapon.

Buck yelled: "Damn you, Pete, give it up!" He cocked the pistol a third time.

Roy got the rifle barrel braced over his knees and pointed at Fyffe. Buck stepped aside. Pete wheezed: "I know you're Fyffe, you sonovabitch, stand still, you bastard!" He pulled the trigger. The Winchester barked. The bullet passed where Fyffe had been, and Roy squirmed to realign his aim. Feeling cold and sick, Buck shot Pete once again—it was like killing a wounded, pain-mad wild boar, but he finally stopped Roy.

The smoking gun still in hand, Fyffe let his arm fall to his side and stood staring at Pete's corpse for a long moment before he heaved a heavy sigh and, as though approaching a cold-sluggish rattlesnake, cocked the pistol once more. He stepped up to Roy and, the weapon at ready, felt for signs of life. There were none.

He eased the six-shooter's hammer and leathered the iron. He said: "You should have killed me in Sycamore Cañon, Pete, or this morning when you had the chance . . . but you wanted to see me sweat, wonderin' when it was comin', and that did you in, didn't it. Well, hell, that's the way of it, I guess, when you let thoughts of revenge outweigh good sense and an opportunity for a quick gun." He looked off into the trees. "Maybe I'll have to keep that in mind myself, won't I, Pete?

"I guess, you bein' an escapee from Yuma, you're worth fifty dollars to Chedan. Least I can do is get you out of the middle of the damned road and save you for him."

He rose, walked to the nearest bedroll, and got a blanket to wrap Pete's body. He dragged the corpse to the side of the road and began to stack rocks over it. When he was done, he went back to where the supplies had fallen, picked up Roy's saddle, and seated it atop the cairn. In case someone came by and made off with the saddle, he knelt and used Chedan's sign. He tied four clumps of grass into knots with their tips pointing to the rock pile. Now he knew he could separate those stones from all the others around here, and so could the Apache tracker.

Finally, he loaded himself with his own saddle, blanket, bedroll, the canteens, and the two Winchesters, nodded once to the grave, then, looked again at the knotted tuft beside the road. Chedan had gone to a lot of trouble to gain his attention and to guide him in a certain direction. He didn't know why the Apache wanted him to go where the signs pointed, but it behooved him not to ignore things.

Lugging his gear, he returned to the grass tuft that pointed toward the trees, turned west, and headed into the forest. He was looking for more knotted grass; instead, he discovered a forked stick shoved into the ground and holding another branch in its Y. That twig pointed straight ahead.

Following silent directions, he walked only a few hundred feet deeper into the stand of trees before another forked stick and branch told him to turn right. Shortly, he came out into a small clearing beside a tiny swift-flowing creek. Barbarossa waited for him there.

The big black mule was tethered by a long single leather

thong strong enough to let the animal know he was tied to something but fragile enough that should he be attacked by bear or puma—or if no one ever came for him—with a little effort, he could break away and escape. The clearing offered water and grass; Barbarossa could have lasted weeks there, if need be. Chedan had left the mule bonnet on but had slipped the bit; Barbarossa grazed peacefully and only raised his head to look in Fyffe's direction when Buck appeared. He knew the man. He went back to nipping grass.

Buck noted the frailness of the string tethering the mule, walked casually toward Barbarossa, and began talking quietly to him. He eased the saddle, bedroll, canteens, and rifles to the ground, and smoothed a palm over the mule's nose and down the black neck before he replaced the bit and ground-tethered him.

Still moving slowly, he situated the blanket and saddle, secured cinches, tied one of the rifles, his bedroll, and bags on behind, slid the other .44-40 into the saddle scabbard, then, with reins looped over his arm, untied the ends of the leather thong and gathered in its length. He would return it to Chedan provided he ever saw the Apache again.

He started to mount but hesitated. Abruptly, he discovered he was shaking, and lowered his head. Eyes closed, he heard his mind ask: *What am I doing here? What do I do now?*

He'd had a good job, a wife he adored, and a beautiful little daughter, but his family was dead, and his colleagues had betrayed him, willing to see him either also dead or incarcerated in Luther Gibbs's stead just so they might be able to retrieve someone else's money. True, twenty-five thousand was more than a substantial sum, but while you could reasonably expect a lack of honor among thieves over that much, betrayal of a law officer by other law officers for it was something else again, wasn't it?

He felt a renewed surge of rage rise into his throat. Betrayed and setup by his own. The operation, if not thought up by, was at least approved by his long-time boss, Lon Humbert, who was in league with Josh Stoner's manager, Wally Lake.

Revenge. That's want he wanted . . . Revenge.

He shook his head slightly and, with Barbarossa's reins still looped over his arm, lowered himself to the grass to sit staring at the rill. No, he'd just seen how a lust for revenge could drive a man. Part of his own gut shakes was that, while as US marshal he'd shot men before, rarely, if never, had he ever had to blast somebody three times at close range to stop them. Roy's lust for revenge had been so strong, it had eaten him up to the point that he was scarcely human any longer.

His head rose. All right, that was it, wasn't it. Not revenge . . . justice. There was a difference. He would set things right. He would catch up with Chedan, wherever the Apache was, on up ahead. Then, the two of them would trail Luther and Josh to the loot, take Gibbs if it had to be over Stoner's dead body, retrieve the money, and then he was going to get some justice. For Steve Larson. For Steve's widow, Rose, and his fatherless children. And for himself! And then . . .

Well, he'd wait and see what the "and then" turned out to be.

He had stopped shaking. He swiveled around on the grass, removed his hat, bent to the stream, washed his face and hands, and drank. Standing, he urged Barbarossa to also drink. While the mule sipped, he checked the load on all his weapons and refilled as necessary. When Barbarossa lifted his head, leaned to nibble his arm and slobber all over his shirt sleeve, he muttered: "Y'know, comes to me I've never heard you make a sound. You're the quietest mule I ever met."

Barbarossa's ample ears tipped toward him. Otherwise, he said nothing.

Buck swung astride and guided his mount back out toward

the road. Once there, he lifted a finger in parting to Pete Roy's cairn before he nudged the mule northward toward the Verde Valley, Jerome on the slopes of Mingus Mountain, and that justice he sought.

* * * * *

Depending on the time of year, Mingus Mountain's visual aspect changed. It could be greened by sparse grass, or golden with blossoming sagebrush and sparked with bright red-and-yellow agave flowers held proudly on woody stalks tall above spike-tipped leaves. Sometimes, the mountain was a blunt lowering cinder cone blotched with mineral ore, colors like an infected wart rising before the sharp-sided, snow-clad peaks of real mountains to the north.

At its southeast spread was the Verde Valley, as lush with cottonwoods and grass as its name implied. Between it and those northern mountains spread another valley ever-rising past orange spires and deep cañons toward a great plateau cut by the grandest cañon of all. To the east and west rose rumpled hills, some forested, some barren, but few holding Mingus's mining appeal.

Cloud shadows turned the mountain into shades of black and dead-furnace orange. Its brilliant oxidized ores—brown iron, black manganese, blue azurite, and green malachite— were used for hundreds, perhaps thousands of years as pigment by the Sinagua, Hohokam, and Tuzigoot Indians to color their clothing, their pottery, and their bodies.

The Indians were interested in paint, not metal. Various dumps holding valuable ores scattered here and there below several considerable holes in Mingus's side and, farther west, two shallower mine shafts. The ancient Indians used stone tools to dig and juniper ladders to negotiate the resulting tunnels. Modern Indians' tools were scarcely better.

Led by their medicine man, Noch-ay-del-Klinne, who had once been a scout for General George Crook in his 1872-73 campaign, and who was now gathering influence among the Apaches with his assertion that all The People's dead would soon arise and drive the white man away, the Chiricahua nevertheless bypassed the six Indah tents and two fragile wooden shacks perched precariously on the mountain's steep side. First things first. They had come a long way to replenish their ceremonial paint supply, for even more wars were in the offing.

Geronimo predicted disastrous times ahead, and he had the "sight." That Geronimo was Spanish for "Jerome," and that they had come near to the white man's town of the same name for their paint pigments meant nothing to them. Maybe, on their way home, merely as a matter of principle, and if they had the time and were so inclined, they would hesitate long enough to wipe out the few miners and one whore who had moved to Mingus Mountain. Otherwise, if the white men didn't bother them, they would leave them alone, because they had better things to spend their energy on—for now.

South, in the Verde Valley, Chedan hesitated only long enough to again tie a bunch of grass into a knot and let Buck Fyffe know he had passed this way. He glanced northward to where two riders broached a rise. Gibbs and Stoner rode at a brisk pace but didn't push their horses. They proceeded with purpose, yet the Apache got the impression the two felt they had time. Or maybe Luther was the leisurely one, and Josh merely kept pace?

Whichever was of no real importance. Chedan flung himself back astride his pony and continued to follow.

Buck, in fact, stopped at Dewey, but not to greet relatives. At the slant-roofed, slab-walled homestead become way station, he refilled his canteens and added to his trail supplies and ammunition. He paid twenty-five cents for a good midday meal of steak, potatoes, squash baked with onions, apple pie, milk, and coffee, and felt a lot better when he left than when he'd arrived. Secondly, there was something homey and comfortable about using an outhouse sporting two adult- and one child-sized hole rather than having to squat behind a bush while on the trail, or over a bucket as in Yuma Prison, yet even that essence of civilization couldn't lighten his mood of grim determination. He had to work at it to keep his mind on justice rather than revenge. It was an effort, but he persevered.

Some two miles down the road between Dewey and Prescott, he hauled Barbarossa in sharply and reined the mule around to walk him back eastward a ways. His lips quirked into a hard smile; he muttered more to himself than to Barbarossa: "Well, now, would you look at that."

The mule's ears flicked backward to acknowledge his voice, but that was all. He didn't care that grass knotted along the roadside pointed to a barely discernable path running off to the right among juniper, sage, and jack pine.

Buck, in turn, didn't know who he was going to meet ahead, or where, but following Apache signposts, he turned Barbarossa onto the scant trail and doggedly pressed onward.

CHAPTER SIXTEEN

Far peaks shimmered with afterglow against an indigo sky, their tips cast into rose by the fading day, but twilight made Mingus Mountain into a squat, seven-thousand-foot-tall demon crouching over valleys deep with shadow. The Apaches picking at sunset-hued color deep in the rocks ceased work, because paint pigment gathered during darkness drew power only from darkness. They needed all the vibrant sun strength they could realize from the magical symbols they would inscribe on shirt, body, and war shield when the paints were mixed with animal fat and then blessed with cattail pollen.

In Jerome, the few miners ate beans not soaked long enough to forestall gassy intestinal disturbances; could they have harnessed tomorrow's farting, they wouldn't have had to spend money on dynamite to blast ore from rock. Meanwhile, the old whore went to bed alone. The men were too tired to seek comfort in her middle-aged arms.

Luther Gibbs and Josh Stoner halted for the night on Mingus's southeastern flanks. They could have rounded the cone and camped with the miners, but Luther preferred not to advertise his presence and to get his cache early tomorrow morning. Then, dawn light penetrated almost to the rear of the ancient Indian digs, and he would be less likely to fall by accident into one of the vertical shafts. Besides, he needed the time to decide how best to dispose of "Jack Stone." Josh had served his purpose as companion on the trip and handy gun in case of Indian attack, but in no way did Gibbs intend to share the loot with him. Neither he nor Stoner knew about the Apaches at the mine shafts, nor that one followed them.

Chedan made dark camp close enough to Gibbs and Stoner to keep an eye on them, but far enough away that his horse wouldn't be noticed. Of course, he knew about the Chiricahuas at the color mines, and suspected that he, those he trailed, and possibly also Buck Fyffe, would meet them. He used the evening to devise a plan he could use to keep people on all sides from getting killed.

Because of his problem with Pete Roy, Buck was a half day behind Gibbs, Stoner, and Chedan. Rather than make camp in the relatively barren, mostly unprotected bowl of the Verde, he halted in the trees and huge rocks at the valley's southern edge. Besides, he couldn't see the Apache tracker's signposts after dark. Better to rest tonight and start out fresh at first light tomorrow.

Meanwhile, he pondered exactly what he would do when he again met up with Luther and Josh. He was aware that there might be Indians somewhere up ahead—Chedan had warned him—but maybe they had finished their redskin business and were gone by now. He decided he would probably have to play upcoming events by ear, again checked his weapons, and turned in.

* * * * *

"It rained all night the day I left, the weather, it was dry. The sun so hot I froze to death, Susanna, don't you . . ."

"Marshal," Josh interrupted Luther's under-the-breath mumble, "I thought you were headed for Prescott. Not that I'm ungrateful for the company, y'understand, but why are you ridin' all the way to Jerome with me?"

The question caught Gibbs off guard. Firstly, he considered that Jack Stone rode with him, not the other way around. Secondly, he was at a loss to give an immediate and valid answer.

Stoner lay back on his left side, braced by an elbow, ankles crossed, his coffee cup in both hands but pistol in instant draw position. He subdued a grin while he watched the outlaw struggle to come up with something believable.

Finally, Luther blurted: "Well, as federal marshal hereabouts, I gotta keep an eye on my territory, y'know."

"Yeah, but you been on the road a long time." Stoner strove to keep his expression serious. "I mean, first you took that miscreant . . . what was his name?"

"Gibbs," Luther muttered. "Luther Gibbs."

"Ah! Right! I mean, first you took Gibbs to Yuma Prison. Then, you rode all the way back. Don't you ever get time off?"

"A lawman's work is never done," Gibbs snapped. He tried to change the subject. "What'd you say you was minin' for in Jerome?"

Josh had never been to the Mingus Mountain mine sites, but he'd heard there was copper, silver, and maybe even gold there. He said it, embellished with: "I got to look the area over close to decide where to sink my first shaft. Uh . . . you have any interest in minin'? . . . Maybe got a little cash set aside you'd like to invest in a sure thing?"

Luther had a lot of cash set aside, but investment was not on his agenda. He planned to take his money and run, spend it on high-living in San Francisco or perhaps even New York, Chicago, or Philadelphia. None of this squandering his take on work—that was the only sure thing here. Good booze, pretty women, maybe a mansion somewhere, a little gambling from time to time . . . He would use that money properly. He said no.

A short silence followed during which Stoner finished his coffee, tossed remains onto the ground, and stored the cup in his carry-sacks. He again lay back, this time with fingers laced across his belly, and asked: "Wasn't Luther Gibbs the one leadin' the gang that stole some twenty- or thirty-thousand dollars from Southwestern?"

"Yep," Luther said shortly.

"Fascinatin'," Josh noted. "I'd be proud to hear how you caught him, Marshal."

Luther gritted teeth. All this conversation was beginning to aggravate him. He wasn't going to admit that it had been his own arrogance or ineptitude that had allowed Buck Fyffe to take him as easy as roping a cayuse caught in a thicket. He answered: "Pure luck, gotta admit it. Gibbs outsmarted us all. He got clean away, and if it hadn't been for a accident, B-B— uh . . . I and ol' Steve would never have caught up with him."

"Where'd you run him down, Marshal?"

"Here, in the Verde Valley."

"Comin' back to the scene of the crime?"

"Well, sort of. Seems he'd got separated from his men. He'd stashed the take and was tryin' to rejoin his gang. Got caught in the middle of the valley. Y'know there ain't much cover here. His horse was about done in, y'know, and two against one . . . well, h-he didn't have much of a chance."

"But he'd already hidden the money? I mean, I hear the law never located it."

"Uh . . . yeah."

"And Gibbs was comin' from the north? You don't s'pose he hid the loot somewhere near Jerome, do you? Is that why you're goin' there instead of takin' your earned ease in Prescott? Be quite a feather in your bonnet could you bring that in. I hear ol' Southwestern is offerin a five-thousand-dollar reward for return of their cash."

Luther snapped: "No, that ain't why I'm headed north! And besides, as a federal employee, I git paid a salary for doin' what I do. I can't claim no reward."

Eyes twinkling, Josh's brows rose. He murmured: "Well, now, Marshal, maybe if we worked together, we could come up with that payload. I ain't no federal employee. You could enhance your reputation, as they say, by locating the stolen money for Southwestern, and I could claim the five-thousand-dollar reward, which would sure as hell help me with my mining operation. Yep, workin' together, we could both come out ahead, right?" He shoved his hat down over his eyes, but not so far that he couldn't still watch Luther, again laced fingers across his belly within easy reach of his sidearm, propped his head on his saddle pillow, and finished: "Sounds like a good plan to me."

"I'll think about it," Gibbs growled, and also turned in.

* * * * *

"Gawddamn," Luther breathed, "there's Apaches all over the place."

Gibbs and Stoner had resumed their journey at first light this morning, had rounded Mingus Mountain's flank, but now hauled their mounts in to scowl up at one of the ancient Indian digs where eight or ten red men went about their business. From the number of ponies staked out nearby, more Indians obviously occupied the dark, narrow hole probing the rock.

Stoner frowned. "Looks like. What d'you want to do, Marshal?"

"Shit, I ain't takin' on fifteen or twenty redskins, I'll tell you that! And look, here comes 'nother one." He and Stoner held their horses behind a bush while they watched the Apache approach.

Chedan had decided that all Indians looked alike to the white man. He had eased his pony well northward—but not so far that he couldn't still keep an eye on Luther and Josh—and now approached the group of Apaches at the mine shaft.

The medicine man, Noch-ay-del-Klinne, squatted on the slope outside the poke mouth, inventorying colors and amounts of gathered pigment. He looked up when Chedan arrived, nodded, and, using the scout's real name Tats-ah-das-ay-go, said: "Quick Killer, we meet again. I thought you said you were doing your part to rid our lands of the invader."

Chedan dismounted, led his horse near the shaman, and squatted a respectful distance beyond the row of leather bags bulging with colored rock dust lined up in front of Noch-ay-del-Klinne. Speaking in his native tongue, he answered: "I got rid of two since we last spoke, Holy One."

"Only two?" The shaman's brows rose. "Well, every little bit helps, the hummingbird said when she pissed into the lake. And when our dead arise from the bowels of the earth, we will reclaim our lands. Why are you here?"

Rapidly, Chedan explained about Buck, Gibbs, and Stoner, concluding with: "I don't know whether the Betrayed is trail-wise enough to see my guide markers, or if he does, whether or not he will understand them . . ."

"Or if he is still alive," Noch-ay-del-Klinne observed. "He may lie dead far south, sent onward by the hands of his enemies."

". . . but if he lives, and if he follows my markers . . ."

"If . . . if," the shaman scowled.

". . . I would be grateful if you and your men allowed Buck Fyffe to continue to live."

Without raising his head, Noch-ay-del-Klinne looked up suddenly. Black eyes glittered obsidian lights from beneath bushing gray brows. "Why? What is the Betrayed to you? He is merely one more white man."

For a long moment, Chedan studied rust-red spires rising at the north far across the valley. Finally, he murmured: "I was there when he discovered how his own brothers used him . . . betrayed him . . . why they chose him and his friend. Rarely have I seen a heart so wounded, yet he pulled himself out of it and now carries on. He has a responsibility and strives to fulfill his duty."

"Humph. I think you like this . . . Buck Fyffe."

"I've grown to respect him. He does what I would do under the same circumstances."

Again, Noch-ay-del-Klinne snorted a humph. Presently, he added: "Perhaps Quick Killer has spent too much time among the whites." Chedan said nothing to that. A short silence held until the shaman sighed heavily. "Very well. Out of respect for you . . . because you work hard for our cause . . . should we meet the Betrayed on the path home, we will not kill him." He grinned abruptly. "Unless he dies on his own out of fear when we approach."

Chedan chuckled. "I doubt that that one will. What about the other two?"

"Will the Betrayed's enemies bring you much bounty should we leave them for you to kill?"

"One, possibly . . . the one called Gibbs. The other seems to be a lawless lawman."

Noch-ay-del-Klinne tipped his head and fingered the

pigment sacks. "I never thought I'd hear myself say it, but . . . at this moment, we have more important things to do than kill two or three white men. I leave them all to you."

"Thank you, Holy One." Chedan rose, but waited to be dismissed.

"Don't make me regret my decision, Quick Killer."

"I'll try not to, Holy One." Taking that as the end of the conversation, Chedan finished: "May we both live to meet again."

Noch-ay-del-Klinne ignored the younger man. He had returned to weighing pigment sacks.

CHAPTER SEVENTEEN

Buck's teeth flashed in his beard when he bared them to a brief grimace of dismay before he hauled Barbarossa in sharply and cast a quick look back the way he had come. It was too far to retreat. Besides, he didn't want to lose the time it would take to flee from the approaching band of Apaches that dawn light picked out when they mounted Mingus's shoulder. He could head off at a tangent, though no ready cover was available out there, either. Or, he could ride straight into them. If they were the Indians that Chedan had told him about, evidently they weren't on the warpath at present. But if they were a different group, that last choice seemed foolhardy to the point of suicide.

He knew they saw him. Indians never missed a thing. Best he head east and try to go around them. He loosened the .44-40 in its saddle scabbard, unclipped the trigger guard on his side-arm, then, keeping a close eye on the Apaches, urged Barbarossa into a running trot toward the rising sun.

An Indian pointed. Buck kicked the mule into a canter. The Apaches shifted their path in an almost leisurely fashion, clearly wanting to intercept him. Swearing softly to himself, Buck again hauled Barbarossa to a standstill.

There was no whooping, shouting, or other threatening activity among the Indians; they merely seemed to want to stop him. It came to him that if these were indeed those Chedan had previously spoken with, perhaps they had some kind of message for him from the tracker. Secondly, if he started shooting at them and they fired back, he was not only seriously outnumbered, but the gunshots could alert Luther and Josh that something was amiss, and he preferred to sneak up on them, if possible. Still, to merely sit and let twenty-five or so Chiricahuas surround him required all the nerve he could muster.

Buck took care to glance from man to man, acknowledging each when they halted around him, but then focused on the oldest of the lot who, from his painted shirt, age, and regal bearing, might be the leader of the band, or at least a person of power. Holding Barbarossa's reins in both hands, but ready for anything, he nodded to the old man. Grimly, he fought down the cold apprehension in the pit of his stomach and didn't speak, but only waited to see what their intent was.

Noch-ay-del-Klinne looked the white man up and down—coolly—before he asked in bad English: "Whachoo name?"

"Buckley Fyffe." Buck was careful to keep his voice low and steady.

"Buck Fyffe?"

"Yes, sir."

"Ah! Buck Fyffe." The old man nodded around at his companions and vented a string of Athapascan before he looked back at Buck and said: "Tats-ah-das-ay-go wait on you north." Without leave, he kicked his pony southward. Casting hard, speculative glances at the white man, the remainder of the Apaches followed.

Buck sat Barbarossa and watched them go. That was strange! And who the hell was Tats-ah-whoever-whatever? Abruptly aware that his brow leaked sweat under his hatband, and feeling like he had just somehow been missed by a rattler's strike, he gently urged the mule into motion.

* * * * *

The sun had not yet reached midmorning by the time Buck rode over a slight rise and saw the huddle of tattered tents and casually thrown together shacks that were barely discernable from the landscape, all clustered near the mouth of a ragged dent in the hillside. Even as he approached, someone shouted, "Fahr in the hole," and men scrambled out into the open. A muffled boom and a blast of smoke-filled dust pursued them out of the shaft.

Vibration dislodged a boulder from higher up the hill; bouncing from up-jut to up-jut, it rolled downward, struck the left edge of one of the shacks, and took the corner support with it as it rumbled on. The corrugated iron roof collapsed on that side, and an overweight woman dressed in nothing but a grimy corset half laced over her camisole, knee-cinched bloomers, and wrinkled black stockings, burst from the door with the same speed the miners had fled the explosion. Grabbing her tousled gray-shot black hair with both hands, she screeched invectives at the men. They paid her no heed; shovels and picks in hand, they hurried back into the hazy darkness of the mine.

Buck snorted a half-laugh at the occurrence, but then his eyes narrowed. The dynamite explosion had startled six or seven horses tethered nearly a quarter mile away; their tossing heads and tugs against their tethers caught his attention. These were Gibbs's and Stoner's mounts, Luther's packhorse, and the horses they had confiscated from Pete Roy, Joe McNair, and the gelding that Buck had used when he'd left Barbarossa with Chedan.

Carefully, he scrutinized the area, looking for the two men, or for Chedan. He saw no sign of the tracker, but supposed both the Apache and his dun pony could be in plain view but blended so well with the landscape that they were invisible. And, perhaps both Luther and Josh were inside some ancient Indian mine. He nudged his mule onward.

The old whore noted his passing. She flashed a snaggle-toothed smile at him, preened her hair with a hand, and flounced a hip in his direction. He acknowledged her with a finger to his hat brim but didn't hesitate—her appearance had about the same effect on him as the saltpeter in his food at Yuma Prison.

On the other hand . . .

He reined Barbarossa around and toward the half-collapsed shack. The whore grinned more broadly, cupped palms under her breasts, and hoisted to reposition their weight over her corset and perhaps increase her cleavage. She dabbed a hand again at her hair when the man halted his mule and dismounted. "Hellooo, cowboy," she murmured.

Once more, Buck touched his hat brim. He said: "Ma'am, uh . . . would you mind holdin' my mule for me until I get back, and then we'l . . . negotiate?"

"Why, not at all, honey." She reached for Barbarossa's reins. "I ain't expensive, if that's what's botherin' you." Buck yanked both Winchesters free of the saddle when the woman began to lead the mule around to the broken side of her shack. She paused to flash a coquettish look back over her shoulder. "Fine-lookin' young gent'man like you, why, I might entertain you free just for the pleasure of it an' then count on your generous nature to do what's right."

"Thank you, ma'am. I hope I won't be long." Buck slid

the strap of one .44-40 over his shoulder and hefted the other before he again studied the ground between him and the horses in the distance.

There was little or no cover, only a piddling rock or two and clumps of low sage. One stately yucca. Period. That meant he would have to walk exposed and vulnerable from here to there.

Well, standing around wasn't accomplishing anything. He set teeth and, with one Winchester at the ready, moved out.

Loose, shaley soil slid and rattled dryly under his boot soles, even though he stepped carefully and as quietly as possible along the thirty-degree grade. As he neared the horses, he saw a man-high, shoulder-wide, morning-lighted shaft some fifty or sixty feet upslope. A man's voice, shouting in a near scream, issued faintly from out of the depths. Though he couldn't understand the words, the tone clearly indicated furious desperation.

What the hel . . .?

Leaning into the upslope and bent near to the ground, the rifle in his right hand and using the other hand as a brace, he scrambled up the hill to approach the mine shaft mouth from the side instead of coming directly up on it from the front—with the sun at his back, he didn't want his shadow to announce his presence before he was ready. As he neared the hole, words began to be discernable from within.

"You gotta help me! . . . My arm is bad broke . . . I can't make the ladder without help! Don't just leave me here, Gibbs! Gibbs, for gawd's sake, give me a chance!"

Buck knew it was Josh Stoner. Whatever had happened to him in there was serious enough to make the marshal forget to call Luther "Buck Fyffe."

Then, Gibbs's voice sneering: "Gonna be nothin' but mummified bones left of you down there shortly, Mistuh Stone.

Enjoy yer privacy whilst yer meetin' yer Maker. I'll say adios, now. Enjoyed yer company as it lasted."

Careful not to dislodge a rockfall, Buck moved higher up the slope to be near the mine roof before he flattened himself against the shale behind him and held the .44-40 tight across his pelvis and thigh, its muzzle pointed downward toward where someone would emerge into the open. He didn't have long to wait. Pursued by shouted pleas for help and screamed curses, and with a leather and metal–buckled money sack in each hand, Gibbs moved briskly out of the poke. He paused to peer toward the scant miners' camp at the southeast, then scowled warily to his left and scrutinized the valley below before he hurried onward.

Buck let Gibbs get far enough from the mine shaft that he couldn't duck back into it before he snapped: "Hiya, Luther."

Open-mouthed, Gibbs whirled to stare up at Fyffe. He gasped: "Allen! What you doin' here?"

"Not Martin Allen, Luther," Buck growled. "Marshal Fyffe."

"Buck?" Gibbs's mouth opened further.

Fyffe twitched the Winchester. "Federal Marshal Fyffe to you, Luther. You're under arrest for fleein' incarceration in Yuma Territorial Prison. Drop those moneybags, and . . ."

"Not ag'in!" Gibbs howled. "You ain't gonna do this to me ag'in!" Satchels flew off to each side as he flung them down, grabbed for his pistol, and lunged to his left.

Buck pressed the trigger on the Winchester. Two shots rang almost simultaneously across the valley until they reverberated, cast back toward Mingus Mountain by sheer walls of red, beige, and white cliffs towering to the north. Luther had snapped a shot at Fyffe and missed. Buck led Gibbs's plunge and didn't miss. Fired from a higher elevation, the big .44-40 bullet plowed into Luther just beneath his left collarbone and continued down through his chest to lodge against a rib. Mortally wounded, he nevertheless tried to again raise his pistol.

Buck slid down the decline and kicked the sidearm out of Gibbs's hand before kneeling beside the man.

Gibbs's blue eyes met Fyffe's. He choked: "Gawddamn you, Babyface, you do this to me ag'in . . ." He gasped a faint laugh. "At least, Y-Yuma Prison ain't gonna git me."

"Oh, yes, it will," Buck said grimly to what was now a corpse. "You're worth at least fifty bucks to my friend Chedan."

"Thank you for your consideration."

Startled, Fyffe leaped upright and jerked the Winchester around to aim at the source of the voice. The Apache tracker had both hands raised in submission and was grinning at him.

Buck gasped: "Where the hell'd you come from?"

"Oh, I been here all the time." Chedan lowered his arms, stepped forward, and bent to check Gibbs's pulse, found none, and continued. "I buried myself up above, there. Thought you might need backup, but, obviously, you didn't." He nudged Luther with a moccasined toe. "Fifty dollars layin' here."

"And some twenty-five thousand layin' there." Buck eased the rifle strap over his shoulder beside the other weapon and moved to retrieve the moneybags. Eastward at the mining camp, gawkers and the whore, who'd been drawn by the gunshots, evidently decided it was safer to mind their own business. They returned to work just as another muffled shout issued from the depths of the Indian mine.

Fyffe held the moneybags out to Chedan. "Keep an eye on these while I see what's goin' on inside there."

Chedan's brows rose. He looked astonished. "You trust me with that?"

"I do." Fyffe grinned. "One, you're an honorable savage. You ain't gonna run off with it. Two, I think you're also just curious enough to stick around to see how this all turns out. So you watch our proceeds here while I take care of that there, then we'll go get us some justice."

"What you got in mind, Marshal?"

"You'll see, Chedan. You'll see." Buck dropped the money at the Apache's feet and addressed the hole in the hill.

CHAPTER EIGHTEEN

The mine shaft held the musty yet dry scent of ancient rock mixed with the metallic tang of mineral ores. Buck's body almost cut out what sunlight there was; he would have gotten down and crawled to increase sight ahead, except that he was afraid he might lay an unprotected palm on a scorpion, tarantula, or some warmth-awakened rattlesnake that had been too sluggish to strike at Luther and Josh. Even so, there was enough light that he could make out stope grooves along the sides of the tunnel where Indians had used stone tools to carve color from successive layers of strata.

The sun was now risen above the mine roof level and subsequently shortened its glow into far recesses. Buck couldn't tell how far back the shaft went because ahead lay an ominous velvet blackness.

He stopped, one hand on the wall beside him, the other on his pistol grip, and put on his Southern drawl. "Hey, theah! Did Ah heah somebody in heah?"

"Oh, thank gawd! Who is it?" The voice seemed to issue from the bowels of the earth shortly ahead of Fyffe.

"Martin Allen, up in these parts from . . ."

"Here! Down here! Be careful, there's a vertical shaft ahead of you with the top of a ladder sticking up. It's easy to fall over!"

"And who are yew, suh?"

"Jos . . . uh . . . Jack Stone. Help! I need help!"

"If theah's a laddah, suh, why doan yew jus' climb on out of that theah hole?"

"The last four or five rungs are gone. There's nothing to hang on to but the side poles, and one of my arms got broken when Gibbs threw me down here."

"Gibbs?" Buck asked. "Who might that be, Mistuh Stone?"

"Gibbs! Luther Gibbs! The one who passed himself off as Marshal Buck Fyffe."

"Is that a fact," Buck commented, then asked wryly: "Naow, whah would that gent do somethin' lahk that to yew, Ah ask yew?"

"Never mind why . . . I'll explain later! Just get me out of here, Martin! Please . . . please!"

"How deep is that li'l ol' hole yer in, Mistuh Stone?"

"F-Fifteen . . . maybe twenty feet."

"Then, yew jus' hol' on theah. I gotta go back out and git a rope or somethin'. I'll be raht back, suh." Buck turned in the narrow shaft and made his way into the light. He said softly to Chedan still squatted beside Luther's body and the money sacks: "I'm being Martin Allen again. You have something handy we can use as a rope? I don't think the tether you used to keep Barbarossa is strong enough to haul Stoner out."

"How long?"

Buck told him.

Chedan nodded, rose, and trotted westward. He vanished around a hump in the mountain's flank and reappeared shortly, leading his pony. He handed Fyffe a well-seasoned lariat. "Here, Martin Allen."

Buck nodded, pulled his hat down to his eyebrows, and

indicated the corpse and the money. "Stand guard again, if you will please, Chedan. I'll be back with Stoner . . . uh . . . Jack Stone."

In the shaft, Buck flung a loop down to Stoner, heaved until Josh could reach the rungs, then steadied the marshal while the man made his slow, painful way gingerly up dry-rotted timbers to floor level. Even in the dimness, Fyffe could see Stoner's white face greasy with pain-sweat when Josh, the rope still looped around his chest, collapsed panting against the wall and clutched his left hand at the bloody sleeve over his right arm before he gasped: "Thank gawd you came by! I'd have died down there. That bastard, Gibbs . . . to shove me down and then just walk off laughing and leave me . . . wait'll I get my sights on that . . ."

"Won' be hard, suh." Buck kept up his fake drawl. "Ah done kilt mahse'f some gent out yondah Ah thought was Marshal Buck Fyffe. He's layin' daid on the downslope."

"Killed him! Why?" Stoner had rested enough now from his ordeal to lean incredulously toward his rescuer.

Buck shrugged. "Ah dunno, suh. He come outta this heah hole in the hill totin' a couple of sacks, took one look at me, and started shootin'. Ah jus' defended mahse'f. Yew think yew can go on now, Mistuh Stone?"

With Buck's help, Josh made it out of the mine to where Chedan waited. At sight of the Apache, Stoner jerked to a halt and nearly fell. Wide-eyed, he croaked: "What's that Injun doin' here?"

Buck took a firmer grip on the marshal. "He'pin' me. This is mah frien' . . ."

"Tats-ah-das-ay-go," Chedan broke in quickly. He slid a warning look at Fyffe; obviously, he didn't want Buck to call him by his well-known nickname. "It means Quick Killer."

"Quick Killer?" Stoner also glanced at Buck. "H-How . . . Where d'you know him from, Allen, a stranger like you are here?"

Buck eased Josh down to sit on the ground. "Met him on the trail. Nevah hurts to have a frien' roun' if need be." His eyebrows vanished totally up under his hat when he raised them at Chedan. "Yew got eny Injun medicine that'll he'p this heah po boy's broke arm, Quick Killer?"

"Perhaps."

While the tracker went to the nearby yucca, used his knife to chop down the tall, dried blossom stalk and sliced off several thick leaves, Fyffe took a closer look at Stoner. The humerus was more than merely fractured; jagged ends protruded through skin and muscle to gleam pinkly-amber in the sun. Buck scowled and shook his head. "Whut was yew doin' in that theah hole, anyways, Mistuh Stone? That don' look lahk no place fer a decent man to be roamin' round in."

Shuddering with pain, his voice weak and unsteady, Josh gasped: "Gibbs was a thief. H-He hid his last take in there. S-Said he would share it with me if I'd keep ridin' with h-him. We went in to get it, but . . ." He swallowed. "H-He went first. I was bringin' up the rear, but he st-stumbled over something, or so I thought, and fell. When I reached down to h-help him up, he grabbed my wrist and threw me down that hole. My arm . . . gawd, my arm . . ."

"Yeah," Buck nodded. "It ain't good, but we'll do the best we can to he'p yew." He and Chedan didn't try to set anything, but merely used the split stalk and stiff leaves tied with saddle thongs to splint Stoner's arm. They then bound the limb to his body with his belt.

While Stoner sat slouched, his legs sprawled, and tried to recuperate, Buck and Chedan hoisted Gibbs's corpse onto his horse and tied it down. After they helped Stoner into the saddle and Chedan was mounted and leading the extra horses, Fyffe picked up the moneybags.

Stoner said quickly: "I'll take those, if you don't mind, Allen."

Buck heaved the bags over his shoulder, grasped Stoner's horse's reins, and, without answering, led off toward the mining camp to retrieve Barbarossa.

Stoner was unarmed; he'd lost his hogleg somewhere in the depths of the Indian mine shaft, and though his rifle was in its scabbard, his right arm was useless and bound to his body to keep it from flopping. As he reached for the shoulder weapon with his left hand, Chedan, slightly behind him, said: "Don't."

Josh stiffened in the saddle. He grimaced at the pain of the broken bones, and met Buck's eyes when Fyffe turned to look at him.

Buck said softly: "Yew jus' set easy, Mistuh Stone. Yew need real doctorin', and me and mah frien' theah will take yew on daown to Prescott foah he'p." And once again, he was more than a little amazed that Stoner didn't seem to recognize him, couldn't acknowledge what he didn't expect to see. If Pete Roy had told them all that Buck Fyffe was out of Yuma Prison, the relationship between his real person and "Martin Allen" didn't appear to register with Stoner.

Josh covered his startlement at Chedan's warning by asking: "What are you doing up here, Allen? Gibbs and I left you and Pete Jones south of . . . uh . . . Dewey . . . as I recall."

"Yup, yew did that." Buck smiled grimly to himself, but didn't turn around. "Not real neighborly of y'all, as I recollect, takin' off with our horses and all. Couldda got us kilt, had them Injuns attacked again."

"That . . . wasn't my idea. Uh . . . Allen, my name's not Stone, it's Stoner. Josh Stoner. I'm a federal marshal out of Santa Fe."

"Is that a fact," Buck murmured.

"Yes. I knew Luther Gibbs wasn't Marshal Buck Fyffe. It was my duty to keep an eye on him!"

"Dew tell." They had reached the edge of the mining camp. Buck handed Stoner's reins to Chedan and grinned up at Josh. "Yew jus' set whilst Ah git mah mount, Marshal Stoner."

It was the smile that gave him away. Stoner choked with certain knowledge: "Buck!"

Fyffe nodded, abandoned his plowboy act, and snapped: "Sure took you a hell of a long time to come to it, Josh. Chedan, if you'll watch him for me, please . . ."

"He's not goin' anywhere." The Apache's green eyes raked Stoner head to toe; there was a wagonload of menace in the look.

Still carrying the moneybags, Fyffe strode to the old whore's half-ruined shack and called: "Ma'am?"

"I'm in here, lovey."

Buck chuckled before he said: "Well, ma'am, something's come up and I . . . won't be able to stay this time. I just came to get my mule, but if you'd like, I'll be happy to pay you two-bits for lookin' after him."

The woman appeared abruptly at the skewed door, expression hard and palm out. "Four," she said.

"Two, and you're lucky to get that." Buck fished in his pocket, came up with a quarter, and dropped it in the whore's hand. "Where's my mule?"

Her enormous breasts jiggled over her corset top when she jerked her head. "Out back. But you come see me any time, lovey."

"Maybe when I get back, ma'am." Buck had no intention of ever returning. He hurried around the side of the shack and located Barbarossa tethered near a pile of rusting, lead-seamed zinc cans. He tightened the cinch and tied the moneybags to his saddle before he mounted and guided the mule to where Chedan kept a close eye on Josh Stoner. He took the reins to the marshal's horse from the Apache and led eastward toward where the trail cut south to Prescott. Another blast of dynamite from the miners' beginning shaft saw them off.

* * * * *

They rode hard and fast across the Verde Valley, and Stoner was in bad shape by the time they reached Granite Creek a mile or so north of Prescott. Fyffe said shortly: "We'll camp here tonight. I want to hit town tomorrow morning."

"Buck," Stoner gritted, "Buck, I need a doctor bad. My arm . . ."

"You can lay around tonight. You'll see a doctor tomorrow."

"What . . . what d'you intend to do, Buck?"

"I got nothin' more to say to you, Josh. Get down, eat, and sleep. That's all that's required of you." Fyffe reached up and yanked Stoner off the horse.

Josh cried out in agony when he hit the ground. Bracing his left hand against the dirt, he looked up at Fyffe and choked: "It wasn't my idea, Buck! I was only followin' orders! Lon and Wally Lake of Southwestern cooked up the scheme. I only followed orders, Buck! Humbert said . . ."

"I don't want to hear it, Josh! Just shut up, and make yourself as comfortable as you can. It'll be resolved tomorrow."

"Wh-What are you goin' to do, Buck? I mean . . ."

"You'll find out tomorrow. Now sit back and shut up. I got nothin' more to say to you, except that both Chedan and I are very light sleepers these days and it wouldn't pay you to try to leave us in the middle of the night." He turned to the Apache. "Chedan, you need any help, there?"

The tracker was slipping bits and watering horses at the

creek. He left Gibbs's body where it was bound across the saddle, and answered: "No. Thanks. I'll keep an eye on my bounty, and you handle yours."

Stoner didn't know when to quit. He said urgently: "Buck, lissen to me. I tell you, none of the scheme to locate Southwestern's money was my doing. Lon and Wally . . ." His words cut off sharply when Fyffe dropped the coffeepot he had in hand and lunged at him.

Seizing Stoner by the collar, Buck knelt on one knee and, teeth bared below blue eyes blazing with released fury, hissed: "I was following orders! Steve Larson was following orders! But there comes a time, Josh, when a man of honor and integrity stops following orders . . . a point beyond which his conscience will not allow him to go . . . if he has a conscience, Josh. I would never have done to you what you did to me, orders or no orders. Steve would likewise have said no. But not you, Josh. Oh, no, not you.

"Well, I got Southwestern's money back. I got Luther Gibbs back. Felix Glover is dead. Gil Root is dead. That leaves Lon Humbert, Wally Lake, and you, Josh, to pay for what you did to Steve and to his wife and kids, and to me for the sake of Southwestern's money. So don't push me, Josh, or you might not live the night out. After all, who's to say ol' Luther didn't shoot you?"

Stoner stared at rage lambent in Fyffe's eyes, heard it thick in his voice, and this time did shut up. He didn't try to escape and succeeded in living through the night.

In the morning, Buck left Chedan and Luther's corpse hidden in the rocks and brush beside the Woolsey Trail between Prescott and Phoenix. The money sacks secured to his saddle, he led Stoner's mount into town.

CHAPTER NINETEEN

Prescott was part cow town, part mining camp and part military center—Fort Whipple, one of the few stockaded army posts in the southwest, raised ramshackle barracks two miles away. The town had been the Arizona Territorial capitol until it lost the designation. In honor of past importance and hope of future glory, it sported an expansive cottonwood-shaded plaza centered by a white-washed octagonal gazebo, a three-story hotel that would have done New York City proud, and an impressive sandstone-block courthouse. Wide dusty streets named Gurley, Cortez, and Montezuma, bordered the plaza. The curbside of Montezuma across from the plaza was aptly named Whiskey Row because it was lined with saloons.

Riding Barbarossa, Buck led Josh Stoner's mount down Gurley Street toward the center of town. Had anyone looked closely, they would have noticed that the man on the horse had one arm crudely splinted and the other wrist chained to the saddle, but because Fyffe held Barbarossa to a slow walk, he and his captive didn't draw much, if any, attention.

Buck turned left at the intersection of Gurley and Cortez,

reined in, and hailed a teenaged boy hurrying along the board-walk. "Hey, son, hold up a minute."

The kid stopped and scowled at him. "Yeah?"

"You want to make four-bits?"

"Doin' what?" The boy moved closer.

Buck nodded aside. "Over there is the post office. I need two pieces of writing paper and a pencil. Can you get them for me? Then, if you have the time, I'll pay you another four-bits to deliver a couple of messages for me."

The boy brightened. "I got the time." He held out a hand.

Stoner abruptly blurted: "That man you're talkin' to is an escapee from Yuma Prison, kid. Run! Get the sheriff, quick! Run!"

The boy looked startled. He poised for a moment, about to flee until Buck grinned and said soothingly: "Pay him no heed, son. I'm US Federal Marshal Buckley Fyffe, and that man is a . . . prime varmint. The messages I want you to carry for me . . ."

"Don't lissen to him, boy! I'm Marshal Josh Stoner from Santa . . ."

"Shut up, Stoner!" Buck's pistol appeared suddenly out of what seemed to be nowhere. He pointed it at Josh.

Stoner's lip curled. "You won't shoot me in broad daylight in the middle of Prescott, Fyffe!"

Buck's smile spread. He lifted brows to the kid. "There. Confirmed who I am out of his own mouth. Are you goin' to get the papers and pencil for me, boy?"

"Uh . . . sure. Uh . . . be right back, M-Marshal." The teen-ager whirled and took off at a run.

Fyffe's openly pointed hogleg was drawing too much atten-tion. He cast a grim, warning look Stoner's way as he holstered the weapon, and snapped: "Hush your mouth, Josh, lest I shut it for you, daylight and downtown notwithstandin'. This is your one and only warning."

"What are you doing, Buck? For gawd's sake, we been workin' lawmen together for a long time, and . . ."

"Evidently not workin' together, Josh. Just have patience. This'll all be over in about fifteen minutes."

The boy came panting back, bearing a pencil stub and two pieces of plain paper. Buck nodded thanks, took off his hat, and, using the relatively stiff brim as a desk, quickly scribbled two notes. He folded the papers and jotted a name on the outside of each, then leaned to hand the finished product to the boy. "This one goes to Southwestern's headquarters. You know where that is?"

"Yes, sir, I do."

"Good. Hand that to Wally Lake personally, all right? This one goes to Chief Federal Marshal Alonzo Humbert over there in the courthouse. Also see that he gets his note personally. Here. Here's a dollar. You've earned it."

Clutching the notes and his earnings, the boy headed for the Southwestern office, again at a flat-out run.

Buck nudged Barbarossa into motion back toward Gurley Street, and led Stoner's horse farther on down toward Whiskey Row—he needed to be able to see the Southwestern office door, but wanted to be less noticeable to anyone coming or going. He saw the boy vanish inside Southwestern, presently reappear, and head toward the courthouse. Not three minutes later, a tall, lanky man, dressed in a black suit meant to make him seem businesslike but that instead lent him the ominous air of a gunslinger, stepped to Southwestern's front office door, hesitated to settle a flat-crowned black hat over white-blonde hair, and cast a hard glance around before he moved onto the boardwalk. He followed the boy toward the courthouse.

Josh breathed: "You told Wally Lake to meet Lon Humbert in Humbert's office, didn't you?"

"Yep."

"What the hell you gonna do, Fyffe?"

"You'll find out." Buck swallowed hard, not from fear but to keep outrage down where it belonged while he watched Southwestern's chief of security cross Cortez and stride at an angle toward the courthouse steps. There was Wally Lake, one of the two men who had all but ruined his life, who . . .

He gritted teeth, swallowed again to keep from unlimbering one of his .44-40s and taking Lake out here and now. He once again nudged Barbarossa into motion.

This time, Stoner didn't say anything. He merely sat the saddle, grasped the horn with his left hand so the manacle Buck had borrowed from Chedan didn't cut his wrist, and waited to see what was coming over the horizon.

Fyffe let Barbarossa amble around the plaza; he wanted to give Wally Lake time to get to Lon Humbert's office. The boy appeared on the courthouse steps just as Lake mounted them, nodded to the security chief, and pointed a finger at the door before he trotted away, his mission accomplished and the dollar safely in his pocket.

Good, Buck thought. That all said to him that Humbert expected Lake. *Very good.*

Wally Lake vanished inside the building. Buck urged his mule and Stoner's horse up to the hitching rail at street level, yanked the moneybags off his saddle, and draped them over his shoulder. Finally, he fished the manacle key out of his pants pocket. He had to try twice before he could hit the keyhole.

Josh noticed it and smiled sardonically. He mistook Buck's shaking fingers for nerves, and commented: "Now that you're here, not so sure of yourself, eh, Fyffe?"

And Buck lost his grip on calm. He opened the wristband

locked through the saddlebow, seized Stoner's good arm, dragged
the man off his horse, and, with a hand still tight on his prisoner, shoved Josh savagely around the hitching rail, up the steps,
and through the doors.

People looked up from their desks and gawked at the two
men when they passed down the wide hallway. One was pale
and stumbling. A handcuff dangled from a wrist; the other arm
was splinted with sticks and yucca leaves and bound to his body
with a leather belt. The second man was paler yet, so white with
what appeared to be unbridled rage that his blue eyes seemed
black by comparison. Some office workers even rounded their
desks to lean out their respective doors and continue to watch.
They had witnessed federal prisoners brought to the marshal's
office before from time-to-time, but neither of this pair appeared
to be lawmen.

Humbert's door was closed. Men's voices in puzzled tones
sounded clearly through pebbled glass inscribed: US MARSHAL.
Buck didn't hesitate. He kicked the panel open, flung Stoner
into the room, and, as he stepped through himself, slammed
the door behind him almost hard enough to shatter the glass.
He saw Lake and Humbert comparing the notes he'd sent to
each. Lake's said:

Have Southwestern's money. Meet me in my office imme-
diately.

—Humbert.

On Alonzo's, he had written:

Have urgent information re: Luther Gibbs case. Will be
at your office in five minutes.

—W. Lake.

An inkwell tipped and spread a blue stain over papers when Stoner sprawled across the top of Humbert's desk. He jerked around to stare at Fyffe as Buck snarled: "There's your Judas, Mr. Humbert." Then he wrenched the moneybags from over his shoulder and heaved them at Wally. "And there's your money, Lake. Count it!"

The note he held fluttered carpetward when Wally Lake dropped it to catch the bags. Both he and Humbert stared open-mouthed at the ragged, trail-filthy, bearded man still by the door. Josh half lay across Humbert's desk until Lon gasped: "Buck? Buck Fyffe?"

"Be careful of him, Mr. Humbert," Josh warned. "I think he's gone loco!"

"And why not?" Buck snarled. "I've been set up by my own friends"—that word reeked of sarcasm—"my partner has been killed . . ."

"Larson is dead?" Humbert scowled.

Voice rising, Fyffe went on. "I've been overcome by owlhoots while those friends watched and grinned, incarcerated in Yuma in Gibbs's place with Stoner's help and your blessing . . . spent time in the Snake Den there . . . Count your damned money, Lake! Count it! Now!" Back still braced against the door panel, Buck drew his pistol and thumbed the hammer. "Do it!"

Lake had recovered from his surprise. Still holding the bags, he began: "Now, Fyffe, there's no need to get excited. I'm sure all the money is . . ."

Buck took a step forward, booted Stoner aside, and, with his pistol hand, swept everything off the top of Humbert's desk and onto the floor. He gritted: "Dump your goddamned money there and count it, Lake! I want you to be sure it's all there. Lon, don't try it! I'm nobody's pawn anymore!"

Humbert's right had been sliding slowly toward his open

jacket front; Buck knew from long past association with his boss that Lon kept a Derringer hidden under his coat. Instantly, the chief lifted both hands into the air. He began: "Buck, now let me explain."

"I heard the explanation from Gil Root, I don't need to hear it again. Count, Lake!"

Gray eyes narrow in his lean face, the Southwestern security chief slowly lowered the moneybags to Humbert's desk and began unfastening buckles. One by one, he dumped the contents onto the polished walnut plane—bundles of greenbacks, and sacks of gold coins. He asked softly: "Where is Gil, Marshal Fyffe?"

"Dead," Buck snapped.

"You kill him?"

"No. Count."

"And Felix Glover?"

"Also dead . . . and no, I didn't kill him, either. Why aren't you counting, Lake? Is there some reason why you don't want to count that?"

Lake and Humbert slid glances at each other before Wally said: "No, of course not, Fyffe. It's just that it takes a while to count this much money, and . . ."

"I got time. You do it, Lake, or I'll do it . . . and I'll use your fingers to tally without your hand attached!"

"C-Count it, Lake," Stoner urged. "You don't know Fyffe! I think he . . ." He lapsed into silence when Wally grabbed a sheaf of greenbacks and did begin to count.

"Out loud!" Buck ordered. "I want to hear it, Lake."

Wally hesitated. A muscle jumped in his cheek when he ground his teeth, but he began again at the beginning. Silence but for the tersely-spoken score fell over the room while Lake counted . . . and counted. When he reached twenty-five thousand dollars, Buck's eyes widened. Twenty-five thousand in greenbacks—but the two coin sacks were still to be opened.

Fyffe whispered: "Keep counting, Lake. Don't stop now. This is gettin' too damned interesting."

Under threat of the readied pistol pointed at him by a man clearly on the verge of losing control, Lake opened the first sack. It held ten thousand in twenty-dollar gold pieces; the other, another ten thousand.

"Forty-five thousand dollars, not twenty-five," Buck breathed. "You filthy sons of bitches, no wonder you let Steve die, tried to kill me or see me put away for years and years in Yuma . . . anything to let Gibbs go free so you could cover your asses and recover your take. You advertise that Luther Gibbs stole twenty-five, when in fact, he got near twice as much, then when you got the money back . . . the twenty-five thousand dollars back . . . you two could split the extra twenty, and if anyone asked about the variance . . . gee! . . . But the outlaw must have gotten more than you originally figgered, and shit . . . who knows what he did with the rest! Josh, how much was your cut gonna be?"

Stoner still sat on the floor where he had landed when Fyffe shoved him aside to clear the desktop. He choked: "A th-thousand . . . and a promotion . . . but I didn't know about this part of it, Buck, I swear to gawd I didn't!"

"Well, no matter." Fyffe smiled grimly. "Mr. Lake, count out five thousand in gold pieces."

"Why! What are you . . .?"

"By God, Lake, count, or you'll wish you had!"

"Do it, Wally," Humbert said softly, his eyes on Fyffe. "I think . . . you'd better do it."

Grimly, Lake counted.

"Put that five thousand in one of those bags, and set it on the edge of the desk."

Lake did it.

"Now, take pen and paper . . . Josh, pick 'em up off the floor and hand them to him . . . and write what I tell you." Buck waited until Stoner found a piece of blank paper and left-handedly slapped it up onto the desk. A pen and a capped, unspilled bottle of ink followed.

Buck said to Lake: "Write . . . "Reward for location and return of twenty-five thousand dollars . . . stolen from Southwestern by the outlaw, Luther Gibbs . . . five-thousand dollars paid to Buckley James Fyffe on . . .'" He glanced at Humbert. "What's today's date?"

Lon told him, but added: "You can't claim that, Buck. You're a federal marshal, and you can't claim a reward."

"Not anymore, I'm not. You fired me more than a month ago when you and Lake dealt this hand and used Steve and me as your jokers. As an ex-marshal, I have as much right to that reward as any other plain citizen. Sign it, Lake, put it on the desk, and step back."

Without argument, the Southwestern man did it. Buck leaned forward, picked up the note, scanned it quickly, folded it against his thigh, and shoved it into his shirt pocket. He confiscated the bag of gold coins and walked backward toward the door to keep Lake and Humbert covered, but hesitated long enough to note: "I figure this pays me for wearin' stripes, havin' my head shaved, and spendin' a night and day in the Snake Den . . . not to mention bein' overcome, beat up, shot, and carted, bound hand and foot, across country by the Gibbs gang. But it doesn't reimburse me for how you . . . my friends and colleagues . . . betrayed Steve and me!" He nodded at Josh. "Get Stoner to a doctor. His arm needs fixin'." He cast a cold smile at the marshal. "And, Josh, I think you better watch your back. You now know too much."

"Buck," Lon began, "there's no need for you to quit. We can work this . . ."

But Fyffe yanked the door open, stepped through, and shut it behind him. He holstered his sidearm. Carrying the leather bag, he strode swiftly toward the front of the building, and, once outside, bolted for Barbarossa. He jerked reins free of the hitching rail, vaulted astride, dropped the money into a saddlebag, kicked the mule into a gallop toward the road where Chedan waited with Gibbs's corpse, and fought down a leaden grimness.

Like Josh Stoner, he also now knew too much. What Lon did or didn't do about it was one thing, but he knew Wally Lake would never just let things lie.

CHAPTER TWENTY

Fyffe met Chedan on the road three miles outside Prescott.

"What happened? Where's Stoner?"

"I'll tell you on the way. Let's get the hell out of here. We got over two hundred miles to go to get back to Yuma with ol' Luther there. We have to pick Pete Roy up on the way, and we probably have hired gunnies hot on our trail. Move, Chedan, or we ain't gonna make the low desert with whole hides!"

Someone had, in fact, made off with Pete Roy's saddle, and if Buck hadn't taken the time earlier to tie grass into Apache sign bundles, they might have missed the spot. They paused only long enough to drag Roy's blanket-wrapped corpse out from beneath its stone cairn and tie the festering remains on the horse behind the one carrying Gibbs's body before they once again headed down the steep, winding Woolsey Trail as fast as was safe for their animals. Their haste wasn't wasted effort.

* * * * *

In Lon Humbert's Prescott office, Wally Lake and the chief marshal cast sick looks at each other. Humbert murmured: "I told you we should never have tried it. I told you it was too chancy, but, no, you went ahead with it anyway and dragged me down with you. Now what the hell are we going to do?"

Lake's expression took on a harder cast. "You weren't reluctant to accept your share, Lon. Don't try to put the whole blame on me. We were in this together from the outset, laddie, so now the only question is . . . what are we goin' to do about your man Fyffe and Mr. Stoner here?"

From the floor where he leaned against Humbert's desk, Josh shoved himself to his feet. His left hand braced on the desk-top, he choked: "I got to see the doctor . . . get this arm fixed, else I'll never use it ag'in. This is my gun hand. I don't get my arm fixed, my career as a marshal is over. You won't help me, I'll make it on my own, but I gotta go now!"

Wally Lake looked Stoner up and down before he indicated the money. "What about this, Josh? What do you intend to do about this?"

Stoner whispered, "I don't give nothin' about your take or your plot, I just gotta see the doctor. Lon gives me my thousand and recommends my promotion like he promised, my part's done. Nothin' more to be said. But I got to see the doctor, now, dammit, now!"

Lake contemplated Josh for another long moment. He studied Lon almost as long. Abruptly, he reached for the paper-bound bundles of greenbacks lying on Humbert's desk and began stuffing them back into the bags. Both Stoner and Lon watched the Southwestern security chief count out seventy-five hundred in gold coins, dump them into a sack, and heft it. He left the other seventy-five hundred lying in glittering disarray on the desk, and as he tossed the bags over his shoulder, he extended a hand to Josh. "I'll help you to Doc Taylor's office."

Beyond arguing, Stoner let Lake support him through the office door. Leaning over his ill-gotten gains, Humbert watched them go without saying anything else. After a heavy, dragging hesitation, he moved to a sturdy mahogany cabinet sitting against the back wall of his office. He unlocked the bottom doors, took out a dry canvas water bag, returned to his desk, and began to drop gold coins through the bag neck.

Done, he secured the cap, stashed the water bag back into the cabinet, and relocked the doors. Despite each individual coin's small size, that much gold was a weighty amount. He decided it was safer not to carry his cache out in broad daylight; he would retrieve the money sometime after dark.

There was no joy in his heart when he picked his hat from the coat tree and followed Lake and Stoner out into the hallway. Josh and the security chief had vanished by the time he gained the courthouse front door.

* * * * *

Buck and Chedan used what road there was until they reached the low desert at the bottom of the escarpment; then, drawing on his knowledge of the trackless wastelands, the Apache led off southwest. They pushed their mounts, dark camping at night, one standing hard-eyed guard while the other slept, taking turns overseeing their mutual safety. Once, they saw a plume of dust far to the southeast.

"The Bedonkohe going home," Chedan noted.

Buck was grateful for that. It meant that at least that was one group of hunters he wouldn't have to deal with.

Their third night out, Chedan was a stark silhouette

motionless against the stars while Fyffe tried to sleep. Buck stared at the blackness around them and pondered why he was heading back to Yuma Prison. He was no longer a US marshal—either Alonzo Humbert had fired him or he had resigned over a month ago. He had five thousand dollars in gold in his saddlebags. That was a small fortune. He had a good mount, even if Barbarossa was the biggest, rangiest mule ever to burden creation. But he also had knowledge of wrongdoing by lawmen in high places, and though neither he nor Chedan had seen them, he knew that either Humbert or Lake or their hirelings were on his trail to shut his mouth permanently.

Chedan had Gibbs's and Roy's bodies to take back to Yuma. The Apache would collect fifty dollars each, plus the one hundred dollars for this particular job. That was two hundred dollars, a goodly sum for an Indian. They could just split up, the Apache take his bounty to the prison and he go his way . . . where?

California. Yes, he'd heard there were valleys and hills ripe for ranching or farming out near the ocean north of San Francisco. He had been raised on a farm in Virginia, he knew land, and five thousand dollars was a more than ample stake. Yet, he proceeded on toward Yuma. Again, why?

Pride. It was a matter of pride, of principle, of honor, and of completing something started. He and Steve Larson had headed for the prison to take Luther Gibbs to his just rewards. There had been a detour in the journey, but he had Gibbs back now, and marshal or not, by God, he was going to finish the job. Then, if he was still alive after Yuma, he could move onward with a clear conscience and no loose strings tying him to the Arizona Territory.

Laurie would approve of that.

Just before he finally drifted off, he whispered: "Goodnight, Laurie. Sleep well, Phoebe."

He spelled Chedan at midnight. Four and a half hours later, they headed out at first light. A half hour into the ride, a whine and a meaty thuck was followed by the sound of a gunshot. Chedan plunged out of the saddle to land face-first on warming sand.

"Shit!" Buck gasped. He hauled Barbarossa in and unlimbered one of the .44-40s as he lunged from the saddle, hit the dirt running, and fell to his knees over the Apache, the Winchester ready. The followers he expected had arrived, though from the lag time between the bullet and sound of the shot, they were still a long way off.

Someone out there was using a Sharps. The "shoot-today-kill-tomorrow" buffalo gun was accurate for at least a mile, some said up to three. Whoever used it could merely sit atop some far-off boulder well out of range of his Winchester and pick him off as easily as they had downed the Apache.

He cast a quick look around before he bent closer and turned the tracker faceup. "Chedan?"

The Apache's green eyes opened. He muttered something in his own language. There was a great deal of blood soaking the left shoulder of his shirt and dusty vest. The big Sharps bullet had gone completely through him.

A second bullet breezed past Fyffe's ear just as he reached to help the Apache up. "Come on, Chedan, that bastard's got our range! We have to get to some cover! Can't sit out here exposed like this!" Buck dropped the .44-40, grabbed the Apache's unwounded arm, and hoisted.

"No . . . no . . . *ugashe!* Get thee hence, Buck. I am dead. Tell Swachingo . . . my wife, Swachingo . . ."

"Shut up, dammit! You're talkin' Quaker, and you're not dead yet!" Fyffe half-dragged, half-walked Chedan to the nearest mesquite thicket, the only cover handy. He eased the Apache to the ground, dived back out for his .44-40, and cursed passionately when another inch-long bullet nicked his hat brim before plowing into the ground beneath Barbarossa.

Knowing that a man couldn't rapid-fire a Sharps, that the shootist had to seat a fresh bullet, then sight carefully, especially over long distance, Buck took advantage of what time he had. He grabbed the Winchester, scrambled to his feet, leaped for the mule, Chedan's pony, and the corpse-laden extra mounts, and made it back to cover before another bullet scattered mesquite twigs.

He breathed to Chedan: "From the angle of those bullets, that bastard's sittin' high somewhere, but where, I sure dunno. Ain't that much high ground around here."

Chedan had recovered somewhat from shock of his wound. He choked: "Apache trick. Stand on horse's rump."

"Not with a damned Sharps. Too much kick. But at least I know it's not Humbert. Lon has sat behind a desk too many years to be that fit. It's gotta be Wally Lake or some of his men. Here, Chedan, as long as we're pinned down under this brush, let me look at your shoulder."

The wound was ugly, but the bullet seemed to have plowed a clean hole through Chedan's shoulder just below his left collar bone. Though bleeding, it didn't appear that any major arteries had been cut nor any bones broken. Buck used part of the Apache's tunic to make pads for the entry and exit holes and unwound Chedan's headband to bind the crude dressings in place. He made a sling for the arm out of the rest of Chedan's shirt and growled: "Sorry, but that's the best I can do for now. You're just goin' to have to last on your own till we can get you to a doctor." He cast a squint through mesquite leaves. "No shots been fired in too long a time. Makes me nervous. Makes me wonder what they're doin' out there. It's too quiet for my . . ."

A slug took down the gelding laden with Luther's corpse.

"Gawddamn!" Fyffe gritted. "Now, they're after the horses!" He scuttled on hands and knees to where Barbarossa and Chedan's dun jittered, and led them deeper into the mesquite thicket. The other horses followed. He was back shortly, still on hands and knees, and snapped: "Give me your knife, Chedan."

The Apache's face was a curious shade of greenish-brown, almost the same color as his eyes. He moved slowly, but drew out his steel hunting knife and handed it hilt-first to the white man. "What are you gonna do?"

"It's obvious we ain't goin' to make it to Yuma with Pete and Luther, but maybe we can get some good out of them. You gather yourself. When I'm done, next time they fire, we are goin' to run like hell!"

Chedan watched Fyffe belly-crawl to the horse carrying Roy. Buck reached the knife to cut the ropes securing the corpse. Gently, he eased Pete free, lowered the body to the ground, and again used the knife to sever ties. Working quickly, he unwound the blanket. Never the most handsome of men, Roy was now a gruesome sight to behold. Not too pleasant on the nose, either.

Buck gritted teeth, shut down his sensibilities, dragged the corpse to where the dead gelding lay still burdened with Luther Gibbs's body, and braced Roy's elbows over the carcass's flank. He jammed his hat on Roy's head before he repeated the process to free Gibbs body from its bindings. Having been dead some few days less than Roy, Luther was in slightly better shape. Buck got Gibbs propped at the gelding's shoulder. He drew his pistol and folded Luther' stiff fingers around the butt so it appeared aimed.

"Toss me that .44-40, Chedan."

The Apache grimaced as he leaned for the weapon. Buck caught the toss, levered himself up between Roy and Gibbs, fired once in the general direction he thought the Sharps bullets had come from, then hastily arranged Pete and the Winchester so it appeared Roy had done the shooting. He was rewarded by a bullet thudding into Roy's body. The impact knocked Pete sprawling. Buck let Roy lay, leaped for Chedan, grabbed the tracker, and all but flung him astride his pony before himself springing at Barbarossa. Grabbing the horn with his right hand, he jammed his left foot into the stirrup, hooked his heel over the cantle, and slid down the mule's side as he shouted: "Ride, Chedan, ride!"

What appeared to be one fleeing man lying low over the saddle, followed by several horses and a mule, all riderless, bolted at an instant run westward, leaving Luther Gibbs's corpse to guard their backs.

CHAPTER TWENTY-ONE

"Got one of 'em." Lloyd Polk slid down from his stand atop the highest available boulder. He sat his mount and nodded to Wally Lake riding a white-stockinged sorrel.

Grim-lipped and narrow-eyed, Lake also nodded. Polk was his sharpshooter, a longtime Southwestern employee who had done a variety of tasks for him in the past, all deeds well paid for and many in the realm of the definitely shady. The third man in the party was Ted Klein, another Southwestern security man. Klein was an ex-Texas lawman run out of Amarillo by irate local citizens for flagrant indiscretion with the parson's daughter. New to the job, he was hopeful that by not being too persnickety in the morals department, he could move up quickly in security ranks.

"Buck Fyffe?" Wally asked.

Polk shrugged. "Can't tell from this distance. Besides, I never seen Fyffe. Wouldn't know him by recognition. All's I got to say is that the one ridin' hell-bent out there looks like some kind of Injun, and you said Fyffe is a white man."

"Well, then, let's go see what we got." Lake touched

gut-hooks to his sorrel's sides. Obediently, the other two men followed.

A mile on, Lake pulled in sharply and scowled ahead. He and his companions had topped a slight rise; he could see clearly to where the dead horse lay, one body sprawled with a shoulder gun beside it, but the other . . .

"Hold up, laddies! Something's . . . not right. There's one hombre pointing what looks like a pistol at us, but he's not firin'. Something odd here."

"You don't s'pose Lloyd got him, too?" Ted put in.

Lake shook his head. "Dunno. In any case, he don't seem to . . . uh . . . You boys spread out to each side. I'll take the middle. Dismount and let's see if we can sneak up on the bastard. I don't need conversation with Fyffe. He stole five thousand dollars from Southwestern, and all I want is him dead and the money back."

"Gotcha, boss." Polk and Klein reined their horses aside, one east, one west.

Lake sat a moment longer, eyeing the situation ahead before he drew his sidearm and likewise urged his mount into renewed motion. He guided his horse to a clump of prickly pear cactus, dismounted, ground-tethered the animal, and, gun at the ready, did a crouching zigzag run from bush to rock to cactus toward where the unmoving man still held a pistol aimed at where he had once been.

What the hel . . .?

Abruptly, a volley of shots rang from the east. Almost simultaneously, the Sharps boomed once from the west. The man behind the dead horse twitched when bullets drove into him, but the wide-open eyes didn't blink. The face didn't change expression. Only the pistol fell from lax fingers to lay on the horse's rib cage.

Still cautious, Lake eased forward just as Polk and Klein came into view. The three of them, weapons ready, converged on the two men at the carcass. Klein stepped forward and nudged Luther with a toe. There was no blood, only a seepage of foul liquid when the body slumped.

"Jesus," Polk whispered, "we kilt ourselves a couple of gawd-damned cadavers!" He scowled at the death-ravages on Pete Roy's face, smelled Luther Gibbs's decomposition. Repeated: "Jesus . . . that's like to make me puke! Who are they, Mr. Lake?"

"I haven't the slightest . . . wait! My God, I believe this one is Luther Gibbs, though who that other man is, I sure as hell dunno!" He shifted his stance to glare into western horizons before he muttered: "That sneaky bastard Fyffe! He left these bodies here to make us think him and another man had dug in behind the horse, all the while he and whoever is with him got away." He jammed his pistol back into its holster, whirled, and bolted for his horse. "Mount up, boys! They're not more than five or ten minutes ahead of us! We'll catch those hombres yet!"

* * * * *

Josh Stoner, his right arm amputated below the shoulder and the wound bound with muslin, as well-tended as possible by Dr. Taylor but still haggard and white, entered the courthouse. He should have been in bed to ease the shock of losing an arm, but anger and outrage wouldn't let him rest. He wore no gun, though a big bowie knife was sheathed at his belt. He proceeded slowly but steadily down the hallway toward Alonzo Humbert's office. He didn't knock at the door but merely thrust it open, stepped inside, shut it behind him, and leaned back against it, his left hand behind him clutching the knob for support.

Humbert was in. He looked up abruptly, obviously surprised at seeing who his visitor was. "Josh! What are you doing here?"

"Come to show you the results of followin' your orders, Lon." Stoner nodded to where pink showed in spots as blood seeped through thick bandages wrapping the stump and stained the knotted shirtsleeve below it.

Humbert's eyes widened. "What . . . happened to your arm, Josh? Why . . ."

"Bones stickin' through the skin festered, Lon. Doc Taylor said gangrene was settin' in. Had to cut it off to save my life." Stoner's voice was rising. "You ever had somethin' cut off, Lon? I'll tell you, laudanum don't help, Lon! You wish you could die before it's over, but are afraid you're gonna. My gun hand, Lon! I'm so gawddamned useless now, Lon; because I followed your orders, I had to have a neighbor button my shirt for me today! Every time I take a leak, Lon, I gotta have help puttin' by pants back together, merely because I followed your orders, Lon!"

"Josh . . . " Humbert's hand eased toward the Derringer under his jacket. ". . . now, Josh, I'm sorry, but that was an accident, you know that."

"Yeah, some accident. Now, what am I goin' to do to earn a living? . . . Sweep out saloons, if I can hold a gawddamned broom with one hand?"

"No, no, of course not, Josh. We'll find a desk job for . . ."

"I'm . . . I was . . . right-handed, Lon! I can't write with my left. You got a pension plan for thirty-six-year-old one-armed marshals? No . . ." Stoner pushed himself away from the door, stepped toward Humbert's desk, and rounded it to stand over the chief marshal. "No, ol' Buck had the right idea when he took his five thousand dollar reward and ran. Last time I saw you, Lon, Wally Lake left you with seven thousand five hundred in gold, your part of the take from this li'l operation. I ain't greedy,

Lon, but you owe me. I'll take three thousand and you keep four thousand five hundred. We split the money. That way, you still come out ahead, and I'll be compensated proper for followin' your orders! Wherever you're keepin' the cache, get it, count it out, and then I'll be on my way. Do it, Lon. It's only fair, Lon."

Humbert's eyes had narrowed during Stoner's tirade. He hesitated briefly before he said in a soothing tone: "You're upset right now, Josh, and that's understandable. I expect you're also in a lot of pain. Things will look better to you in a day or two, then you come back, and we'll talk again. But for now, Josh, let me help you back to your . . ."

"No! Uhn-uh! I want my money now, Lon, or I'll blow your and Lake's scheme wide open. Let Judge Hauser and Sheriff Danforth in on what you and . . ."

"Oh, you wouldn't want to do that, Josh." A vein began to beat noticeably in Humbert's temple. His voice lowered dangerously. "That wouldn't do any of us any good. If you stop and think about it . . ."

"All I've had to do these last three days is lay and think! About my lost arm! About my lost career! About my lost future!" Josh's left palm shifted to the hilt of the bowie knife. "Fork over my rightful share, now, Humbert, or . . ."

Lon's hand appeared from beneath his open jacket front. Stoner didn't know Humbert as well as Fyffe did; he wasn't prepared for the Derringer suddenly aimed at him. His mouth fell open when Lon breathed: "And how can I be sure that when you run out of money, Josh, you won't be back to ask for more, eh? Now, if you'll be reasonable, so will I. You go home and reconsider, Josh. In fact, go back to Santa Fe when you're able, and feel lucky to still be alive."

Stoner choked: "You bastard! You ain't gonna give me my bounden due at all, are you? I earned it, by gawd, and . . ."

"Josh," Humbert waggled the Derringer in warning, "simmer down, now."

"You lyin', cheatin' bastard, you made me into a one-armed beggar but you won't . . ." Stoner drew the knife and lunged at Humbert.

Weakness and pain made Josh slow. When Lon pressed the trigger on his Derringer, the bullet slammed into Stoner's chest just below his heart. Humbert could have evaded the dying man's attack had he not stepped back and tipped his chair. Both he and the furniture crashed to the floor, and the knife buried hilt-deep into his belly.

Driven by anger, or hate, or lust for revenge, Stoner summoned enough strength before he died to support himself on the ravaged stump of his right arm, yank the blade free, and drive it into Humbert's throat.

Drawn by the gunshot, office workers raced down the courthouse halls to the chief marshal's door and burst into the room to see two bodies sprawled on the carpet. Josh's fingers were still locked around the knife hilt, and the gawkers wondered why a marshal would murder his own boss.

Still hidden behind cabinet doors, the gold wouldn't be discovered for days.

* * * * *

Buck guided Barbarossa close to the Indian pony and grabbed at Chedan to keep him astride the dun when the tracker started to slide out of the saddle. It sort of surprised Fyffe; somehow, he'd always thought—if he had thought about it at all—that an Indian wouldn't be much bothered by something like a gunshot wound that wasn't immediately fatal, but he guessed Apaches were people just like whites, after all.

He knew Chedan couldn't go much farther. He also felt that his corpse barricade probably hadn't fooled their pursuers for long, and that whoever those men were, they were hard on their trail once again. Grimacing, he made a quick decision.

Still half supporting Chedan, Buck reined the mule into the pony to turn the dun toward a clump of tamarisk, creosote bushes, and two tall saguaros, the right-hand cactus sporting three elf owl nest holes straight down its middle. He let go of the Apache and seized the pony's reins to lead him into the thicket, pulled to a halt, and dismounted. Chedan was almost a dead weight when he eased the man to the ground and lay him in the shade.

The Apache's green eyes met his blue. "Don't . . . understand. I'm wearing my *izze-kloth*. No . . . no bullet should have struck me."

Buck frowned. "What's an izze cloth? Your headband?"

"N-No. Medicine cords. These." Fingers of Chedan's right hand touched the stone-, feather-, and amulet-laden strings slanted across his chest.

"Oh, come on, Chedan, you were educated by white men. You should know that's just superstition."

"*Tah unzhoda.* Too bad," Chedan muttered.

Fyffe didn't comment further on his opinion of the effectiveness or lack thereof of Apache talismans. Hurriedly, he got a canteen from Chedan's saddle and the Indian's carry-sacks. He tied the pony and the extra horses nearby before he knelt and lay the supplies beside Quick Killer. "Listen, Chedan, you hole up here and rest. I'm goin' to circle around, hit our back trail, and see if I can come up behind whoever it is who's after us. Maybe I can take 'em out instead of them ambushing us again, okay? You lay low here until I get back. With luck, I won't be long."

"Take my pistol. You left yours with the dead." Chedan started to draw the weapon.

"No, I've got one .44-40 left and ample ammunition. Keep that to defend yourself, if need be. Don't hesitate to shoot to kil . . ." He flashed a grin at the Apache. " . . . unless, of course, it's me comin' back."

"*Ashoog*," Chedan gasped. "Thank you."

Buck nodded and rose. Before he mounted, he broke a tamarisk branch, and then he leaped into the saddle and, leaning down, carefully brushed-out hoof sign from where Chedan lay hidden until he came to where they had turned aside. Discarding the branch, he kicked Barbarossa southward a ways, then eastward, then north to circle around behind their attackers, and now he hunted the hunters.

CHAPTER TWENTY-TWO

Because the mule was so tall, Buck bent tight against the roached mane so not to skyline himself yet still be able to see over or through the feathery tops of mesquite, tamarisk, and creosote bushes. Without his hat, the summer desert sun beat hard on his skull, but his hair had grown to a reasonable length now, and, though noticeable, he knew he could survive the heat.

Not five minutes on, he saw movement to his left. Quickly, he reined Barbarossa to a halt behind some brush, readied the .44-40, and frowned through leaves at those approaching. Presently, his lips thinned in his beard.

Wally Lake and two men he didn't know. The trio moved at an easy but purposeful canter, their eyes on the dirt as they followed his and Chedan's tracks.

All right. He wasn't going to try to best three men in a face-to-face shootout, especially when all he had to work with was the shoulder gun. Though it went against his grain to ambush a man, there were times like this when you had to set your principles aside.

He noted the one who carried the Sharps. A powerful gun,

but slow. The second man was also armed with some kind of a rifle or carbine carried in the crook of his left arm. Lake packed a full twin holster.

He murmured to Barbarossa, "Easy, now, mule," as he sighted on the man cradling the carbine, and his well-aimed bullet cut short Ted Klein's hoped-for Southwestern security career.

Instantly, their weapons unlimbered, both Lake and Polk hauled in their horses, jerked around to glare in the direction the shot had come from, and blasted away at bushes. Buck slid down the offside of the saddle just as the two hunters also leaped to the ground and slapped their mounts away—they could tell that the gunshot had come from somewhere very nearby and its general location, but that was all.

Crouching, his eyes on the Southwestern men, Fyffe moved northward a few paces. He levered another cartridge into the .44-40 as quietly as he could, though because of the ominous silence in the aftermath of the fusillade, the slide of the bullet casing against oiled metal seemed so abnormally loud to him that he flung himself flat to the sand. In fact, it drew more fire from the Sharps—the bullet scattered leaves shortly to his left.

Buck rose to one knee, sighted slightly upwind of the puff of smoke rising through mesquite branches, and squeezed the trigger. He was rewarded with a yelp, cursing, and scrambling sounds to the southwest. He straightened, saw Lake and the sharpshooter bolting for their horses, and snapped another shot off at them. Lake's hat sprang from his head to let sweat-stringy white-blonde hair gleam under the sun, but both Wally and his partner made it to their mounts and thundered away to vanish into the brush before Buck could get another decent shot off.

Fyffe eased from beneath his cover and moved cautiously to where the man he had shot lay. He paused a long moment, scrutinizing the body to make sure the hombre wasn't merely playing possum. When he could make out no movement and was fairly sure the others had gone, he stepped forward and toed the man over onto his back.

Dead. Good and dead.

He quickly relieved the corpse of his armament; a Model 1874 .44-40-caliber Remington handgun that he noted with satisfaction would take cartridges from his own .44-40 shoulder weapon, and a much-used sixteen-round lever-action Henry rifle. He found the magazine full, but scant reload of .44 cartridges in the corpse's shirt pocket.

Now well-armed, he hastily went through other pockets, let a full money clip lay where it was, and read from a small card tucked in a thin wallet that the man had been one Theodore G. Klein, Southwestern Security. He dropped the card and the wallet back into the pocket, and rose. He had been right. Three—now two—Southwestern men were after him.

He started to return to Barbarossa but hesitated. He'd left his own hat on Pete Roy's dead head, and he needed one. Klein's pearl-gray flat-crowned felt lay a short distance away. He strode to it, slapped dust off it, and tried it on. A tad large, but when his hair grew out a little more, it would be all right.

Grimly, he walked back to where Barbarossa waited and slid the Henry into the saddle scabbard. The .44-40 in one hand, the mule's reins in the other, he warily moved on foot toward the cluster of tamarisk, creosote, and saguaro where the Apache tracker lay hidden. At the edge of the copse, he said softly: "Chedan, it's me. Don't shoot."

"I won't if you don't," the Indian muttered. When Buck appeared, he asked: "How many are they?"

"Were three." Buck shifted the .44-40 to his left hand along with the reins, bent for the canteen, and drank before he finished. "One down, one grazed. They ran. I just came back to let you know I'm goin' to leave my mule here and track them down on foot. I don't know when I'll be back . . . if I come back. You goin' to be all right by yourself for a while?"

"Yeah. All I need is a little rest. Where'd you get the hat?"

"Let's just say it wasn't bein' used anymore." Buck dug jerky out of his saddlebags from beside the poke of gold coins and stuffed the dried beef into a hip pocket. Without another word, he turned and left.

Fyffe knew which way Lake and his segundo had gone, and figured they hadn't run too far. Eyes alternately scrutinizing the landscape around him and scouring the dirt for hoof sign, he walked west until he located the Southwestern men's path. Cautiously, he began his stalk.

He thought: *If I was a hunter who suddenly became the hunted, what would I do? Try to turn the tables back the other way as soon as possible, that's what. I would leave my compadre behind somewhere along the trail, lead his riderless horse with me to look like we both carried on...or step aside myself and hope to waylay my pursuer.*

With that in mind, Buck moved into denser cover. Keeping one eye on the hoofprints, he also watched for signs that someone had dismounted and waited hidden for him to pass. Evidently, Lake had snagged Klein's mount, for the hoof sign of three horses scarred the dirt.

Cautious as he was, some ten minutes later, just as he caught a flash of sunlight on metal in the brush on the other side of the hoofprints, a shot rang out. The big Sharps bullet struck his Winchester at the junction of stock and barrel, shattered the weapon into two pieces, and left his hands numbed. *Damn them, they've done exactly what I surmised they would do, but they still sure caught me by surprise!*

Heart pounding, and wondering where the second man was, Buck dropped flat and clawed the Model 1874 from its holster. Though the pistol's front sight had been filed from its six-inch barrel to expedite a quick draw, he knew the damned handgun didn't shoot straight for more than about thirty feet, which meant he had to get closer to the marksman over there.

As silently as he could, he belly-crawled across gravelly sand and fallen twigs for a few feet before he rose to a crouch. Hunkered low, he readied his weapon for a quick shot. He burst from behind a mesquite, dashed to another, and flung himself under that.

He hadn't fooled anybody. A second bullet creased his shoulder blades. He felt hot blood begin to spread into his shirt. Merely nicked, he nevertheless shouted in pain and collapsed onto his right side, his back toward where the shootist hid—he wanted his attacker to see the blood and think him mortally wounded. He knew he was taking a desperate chance, gambling that neither Lake nor his partner would shoot him again before approaching close enough, but felt he had to risk it. He tucked the handgun under his left arm folded over his chest, with only the barest end of the barrel exposed, let the hat half fall when he dropped his head to the sand, and froze.

It was a lengthy wait. Watching through his eyelashes for men or their shadows, he lay unmoving for what seemed to him to be at least fifteen minutes, though the time was probably a lot shorter. The grate of a boot heel against sand behind him made him have to fight not to jerk around and fire. He breathed shallowly and silently through parted lips, kept his eyes mostly shut, appreciated that skin over his back still bled to add to the illusion of a mortally wounded man, and kept waiting. It was difficult not to somehow react when something prodded him in the spine, but he managed to remain motionless.

Again, the nudge. Still, Buck didn't respond. Presently, a hand grasped his shirt to turn him over onto his back, and the business end of a Sharps barrel pressed against his throat.

Eyes hard on Fyffe, the man opened his mouth to shout: "Hey, Wally, I got . . ."

Buck pulled the trigger on the weapon tucked under his left arm and thrust himself aside just as the Sharps discharged, its trigger squeezed by a spastic convulsion of the hands holding it. The bullet plowed into sand where Fyffe had been. Buck sent a second bullet into the stranger even as the man dropped the buffalo gun and plunged backward into mesquite branches.

Not inclined to take the chance his would-be killer had, Fyffe rose to his knees and sent a third bullet into the man before he leaped up, scooped up the Sharps, lunged for the body, and ripped open pockets until he came upon a handful of cartridges. He shoved the ammunition into his own shirt pocket, retrieved his hat, again readied the revolver, and then, with the Sharps in his left hand and the sidearm ready in his right, turned and cat-footed it away, again leaving the body of a man he had just killed lay for the scavengers to clean up.

Whoever the hombre had been, he wasn't Wally Lake. There had been three men in the pack after him and Chedan. He'd now gotten rid of two. That left Wally Lake somewhere out there, and as vultures went, Wally was as mean and dangerous as Pete Roy and probably a lot smarter. With Chedan down and the Southwestern security chief's two hardcases eliminated, that left just him and Lake to finish this thing alone.

A small, nasty voice in the back of his mind said: *This is what comes of learning things you shouldn't know about men in high places, ain't it, Buck?* He had gone into law to try to protect the innocent and help bring some order to the wilderness, but if stealing, cheating, lying, betraying your friends, and indulging in murder were what was required in order to advance up the ranks in any business, even in—or especially in—law, he was glad to be getting out of it. He wasn't interested enough in prestige and title, or even in money, to make him want to live like this. In fact, that farm or quiet ranch in California was beginning to look better and better all the time.

Well, Laurie, he thought, *this is it, ain't it? This doesn't go well here, then I'll be seein' you and Phoebe soon, won't I? If that turns out to be the case, I hope you have a nice place set up for me real close to you.*

Once again, he melted into the brush.

CHAPTER
TWENTY-THREE

The hoofprints continued on southward for some five hundred yards before they bore east. Ahead under a tamarisk, Buck could see the shadowed outlines of three tethered horses, but he wasn't foolish enough to expect that Lake was with them. No doubt the chief Southwestern security officer had done one of two things: moved aside to some likely spot and dug in, or was even now drifting through the brush looking for him.

Wally had two sidearms, maybe also a rifle. He had the Sharps—not good for rapid fire—and the inaccurate Remington handgun. It seemed to have come down to who got first drop.

Buck settled under a bush, froze, and listened hard. A slight breeze rustled leaves. Somewhere far off, a hawk screeched. At his feet, a large hairy gray spider did silent but desperate battle with a buzzing tarantula hawk wasp. And over there, with only the faintest rasp of dry scales on drier dirt, a seven-foot-long diamondback hurried from shade patch to shade patch to get out of the heat. Nothing else.

He made a wry grimace. He knew that despite the silence, Wally Lake was out there somewhere merely waiting for him to get careless. All right. They could chase each other around the desert till doomsday, unless . . .

That last Southwestern man he had downed had been the one carrying the Sharps. He didn't know the hombre's name, but maybe that didn't matter. Quietly, he lay the buffalo gun on the sand and drew his sidearm. After a narrow glance all around, he pointed the hogleg at the sky, fired two quick shots, dropped the weapon, grabbed the Sharps, and squeezed off one shot. He let a couple of heartbeats pass before he yelled: "I got 'im, Wally! I got Fyffe! He was goin' after the horses, but he's down and dead!"

And a voice answered: "Goddamned good! Where are you, Polk?"

Polk, was it?

As he reloaded the Sharps, Buck replied loudly: "'Bout a hundred yards due west of the horses, Mr. Lake!" He propped the buffalo gun against his knee and rapidly replaced spent shells in the handgun. That done, he pressed deeper into the mesquite, took up the Sharps in his left hand, thumbed the hammer on the hogleg, and again listened.

Presently, footsteps sounded from his left. Then, through the leaves, he saw sunlight gleam on Lake's blonde hair. The security chief moved past him to some twenty feet on toward where the horses waited before he stopped, looked around, and presently called: "Lloyd? Polk? Where are you, Lloyd?"

Buck eased upright, stepped out of mesquite branches, drew a good bead on Lake, and said quietly: "Right behind you, Wally."

Lake whirled, mouth open and hands dipping for his leathered sidearms. He aborted his draw on his own when he saw that Fyffe already had a cocked weapon pointed at him. He gasped: "Jesus! Fyffe! Wh-Where's Polk?"

"Dead some ways back, Wally. Now, the question is . . . what are you and me goin' to do here and now? You like to give it up, go home, and enjoy your take, or are you thinkin' to keep huntin' me to shut my mouth?"

Lake's eyes flicked from Buck's cold blue glare to the Remington, and back. He licked lips. Still didn't move. His fingers were only inches from his pistol grips. He said: "That . . . depends on you, Fyffe. What d'you intend to do with what you know?"

"I'm out of it, Wally. I got Luther Gibbs's and Pete Roy's corpses that I'm gonna take back to Yuma Prison where they're s'posed to be . . ."

"Those two bodies you left with the horse carcass?"

"Yeah. I got my five thousand dollar reward for gettin' Southwestern's money back for you. What you and Lon do with your ill-got gains is up to your questionable consciences. But I ain't law anymore. Like I said in Prescott . . . Humbert fired me the day he decided to use Steve and me as jokers in this deal, so . . ."

Lake's lip curled. He interrupted: "So you'll just go your way and forget any of this ever happened?"

"That's my intent."

"Never say nothin' to nobody about how much Luther Gibbs did or didn't get during the robbery?"

"You got it."

"Like hell!" Lake lunged aside even as both hands finished his draw.

Buck wasn't caught unprepared. He had expected something like this. Even so, his own dive back into the mesquite nearly spoiled his aim, and Lake's plunge almost let him evade the .44-40 bullet. Buck's shot caught Lake in the hip instead of the chest, but one of Wally's bullets also struck Fyffe just below the scar where Luther had "set the stage" a month ago.

Oblivious to the wound, Buck rolled out of the brush and onto bare ground just as Lake fired at him again. At this close range, it was practically impossible for either of them to miss. Fyffe's snapped shot caught Wally in the left wrist, sent one pistol to the dirt, and Lake's own bullet knocked the Sharps out of Buck's grasp.

There was a brief hesitation. Lake sat on the ground. His hip wound made his left leg useless, and his left wrist was shattered, but he still aimed a pistol at Fyffe with his right. Buck got to his feet, his forearm pressed against the hole in his side, the cocked Remington aimed dead-on at Lake.

Fyffe said: "Look at us, Wally. What are we doin' here? We goin' to just stand here and shoot each other until one or both of us is dead? If so, then you won't be able to enjoy your take and I won't use mine. We can call it a draw and each of us go our way peaceful. I'm not inclined to kill a man merely for the sake of . . ."

"Shut up!" Lake's face was nearly as white as his hair. The gun he held on Fyffe wavered erratically, but he still held it pointed as best he could. "I c-can't let you live, don't you see that? I let you live, one day you'll decide you maybe oughtta do the right thing and turn Lon and me in. Gotta kill you! Gotta do it!"

Buck's expression went ugly with bitterness. He eased the hammer on his sidearm, leathered the weapon, and let his arms drop to his sides. "Then, do it, dammit. You gonna pull the trigger or try to talk me to death? Go on, pull the gawddamned trigger, Wally! Do it, you sonovabitch!"

Lake's mouth fell open. Eyes wide in a stunned gape, he gasped over the bobbing pistol: "You want me to kill you?"

"At this point, I don't give a shit, Lake. I got a wife and daughter waitin' for me on the other side, and I wouldn't mind seein' them again at all. But if you're goin' to shoot me, you'd better hurry it up before that big ol' rattler you're sittin' next to takes it in his mind to strike."

Lake began: "Ahhh, don't try to pull that on . . ." His voice choked abruptly when motion to the side caught his eye. It was that seven-foot-long diamondback Buck had seen earlier, coiling in the shade. Lake jerked around to look, then tried to fling himself away. His movement kept the snake's fangs from his face; instead, they sank deep into his throat.

Wally screamed a hoarse shout of pain and horror, dropped his pistol, seized the snake with his working right hand, and ripped it loose. He flung it aside—the snake recovered and vanished rapidly toward the shadow beneath a sizeable rock.

Lake made undefinable noises as he grabbed at the bleeding holes in his throat. The garbled sounds evolved into: "Burns! Gawd, it burns! Don't just st-stand there, Fyffe, help me! You gotta do s-somethin' to h-help me!"

Buck stared dispassionately down at Lake. Presently, he walked forward, bent painfully, and retrieved Wally's pistols. He moved back a step or two and, holding the sidearms in his left hand, squatted on his heels. He could see Lake's throat already beginning to swell.

He said: "I could lance the wounds, Wally. I'm a tad shaky, though. Might accidentally cut your windpipe in the process."

"The pain," Lake whispered. "Burns! Gettin' dizzy. Buck, don't let me die like this . . . sh-shoot me, Buck. Do somethin'!"

Fyffe stayed sitting on his heels. He murmured: "I recall my partner, Steve Larson, dyin' just like this, Wally. You recollect Steve, don't you? . . . Nice young man with a wife and two young'uns. Had the lung fever, they say, but still had a ways to go before he passed on . . . until you and Alonzo sent him and me out as pawns in your game of chance.

"Rattler got him in the leg. Ol' Luther, he said he'd never

seen anyone go so fast from a snakebite. Said that rattler must have got Steve right in a vein. I do believe you're goin' to beat Larson's record, though, Wally. Do believe you are."

"Buck! Buck, take the money! There's over eight thousand in my safe back at h-headquarters, Buck, just h-help . . ."

"I don't want your money, Wally. I got my own. And what I have I earned honestly, not thievin' it out from under my superiors' noses or sendin' men out to die or wrongfully to prison to get it. I don't want your money, Wally. You keep it and see how much good it does you."

Over the next fifteen minutes or so, Fyffe sat and watched Lake grow paler. He saw the man vomit and flop weakly on the ground as the venom did its work. The wounds in the Southwestern security man's wrist and hip had begun to seal, but anticoagulants in the snake's poison burst them anew. It was a toss-up whether swelling of his throat choked him or whether Lake bled to death, but he did, in fact, beat Steve Larson's dying time by a minute or two.

"'Vengeance is mine, sayeth the Lord,'" Buck whispered. That was a lesson he had learned from Pete Roy. As far as he was concerned, except for one or two final items, this thing was done. He wasn't going to go after Humbert. He would let Lon's own fate take care of him.

Wearily, he rose and looked down at the wound in his side. It was painful but, unless something vital had a hole in it inside, inconsequential. He let Wally Lake lay, more fodder for the scavengers, walked to where the three outfitted horses were still tethered to the tamarisk, slowly mounted Lake's sorrel, and led the other two back to the thicket where Chedan waited in hiding.

The Apache wasn't there. Neither was his dun pony, though Barbarossa and the extra mounts were still tied to branches.

"Chedan? Chedan!"

"No need to shout, Buck. I'm right behind you."

"Damn . . . stop sneakin' up on me like that! You could get shot again, sneakin' up that way! What the hell are you doin' up and ridin' around, anyway? You're s'posed to be resting!"

Chedan shrugged carefully. "I heard gunfire and thought maybe you needed help. Once again, I see you didn't. How bad are you plugged?"

"Not very. How's your shoulder?"

"I'm goin' to live. Why?"

"'Cause we're goin' back and get ol' Luther and Pete Roy, then move on to Yuma."

Chedan looked at him as though Fyffe was the snake that had bitten Lake. "What? You're crazy! Those bodies are so far gone, they'll draw every coyote, puma, and vulture in the territory! I'm not goin' to touch 'em again!"

"Then I'll do it myself, dammit. They're worth fifty bucks each to you, and I am goin' to prove to prison authorities that I'm Buck Fyffe, not Luther Gibbs. Now, if you're up to it, come along. Elsewise, wait here, and I'll be back."

Resigned, but muttering under his breath that all white men, and especially one named Fyffe, were loco, Quick Killer went along with it. Six days later, they delivered Gibbs—almost two months late, but finally—to Yuma Prison, and returned Pete Roy.

Godfrey McHugh, the turnkey, ordered both bodies promptly incarcerated six-feet-deep in the relatively new cemetery, while the superintendent handed Tats-ah-das-ay-go two hundred dollars in gold coin and said: "Glad to see you finally back, Chedan. We had another break last night. Will you help track him? We think he headed for Mexico."

"No," the Apache said, and turned green eyes eastward. "My wife waits for me in the White Mountains. My sons need guidance now, and my daughter must have a father. I am no longer a tracker of white men for white men."

"Sorry to hear that, Chedan. You are . . . were . . . our best. Well, good luck to you, then."

"Thank you." Chedan turned to look at Fyffe.

Buck nodded. "My job here is also done, sir. You take it that I'm not Luther Gibbs?"

"Yes, Marshal. And good luck to you on your next assignment."

Fyffe snorted a half laugh. "I'm not a US federal marshal anymore, sir. Like my friend, Chedan, I've also quit manhuntin'."

"Oh, well, then . . ." The turnkey had returned to the office. ". . . maybe you'll stay on as a prison guard, Mr. Fyffe? We could use a man of your caliber here."

"No, thanks." Buck shook his head sharply. "When it comes to dealin' with packs of varmints, I've had enough of that to last me a lifetime. No, I'm headin' to California. Got my heart set on a nice farm or a ranch and maybe a good woman and a passel of kids to go with it. So I'll say goodbye. Gotta tell you, though, bein' in your prison was an . . . experience.

"Oh! By the way! I've come to like that ol' mule, Barbarossa. Can I buy him from you?"

The superintendent chuckled. "No. Accept him as our thanks for a job well done, Mr. Fyffe."

"All right! Thanks. Uh . . . Chedan, walk out with me."

Outside the superintendent's office, Buck retrieved his mule, picked Wally Lake's sorrel and, out of sentimentality, Steve Larson's gelding, from the string of horses tethered to the hitching rail. He fished in his saddlebags, brought out the sack of gold coins, counted out five hundred dollars' worth, and handed it to Chedan. "Together with these fine riding horses and the two hundred you just got from the prison, here, this ought to finance your retirement pretty well, my friend. Stay home with your family, Chedan, have six or eight more sons, and live to get gray hair."

Quick Killer took the coins. He said: "Ashoog, Buck." He cast a speculative look at Fyffe before he added: "Y'know, you're the second decent, honorable Indah I've known in my life."

Buck's brows rose. "Oh, yeah? Who was the first?"

"My mother. *Yalan* . . . goodbye, Buck Fyffe." Leading his remuda, Tats-ah-das-ay-go headed east.

Chedan's mother was a white woman? Well! Astride Barbarossa, and leading his backup mounts, Buck began to follow the Colorado River northward.

* * * * *

In Ehrenberg, Fyffe lodged his animals in the local livery. Lugging his saddlebags, he signed in to the hotel before he went to make some purchases.

At Morris Goldwater's Mercantile Store, he bought two new shirts, two pairs of pants, underclothes, a trail duster, shotgun chaps, and refreshed his trail supplies and ammunition. He also purchased a small but sturdy box and a length of twine. At the meat market, he obtained a square of butcher paper.

Before he did anything else, he put five hundred dollars in gold inside the box along with a brief letter to Rose Larson telling her she was a widow, that Steve had died snake-bit, and then lied to say that he had given her husband a proper desert burial. He wrapped the box with the paper, secured the whole thing with well-tied twine, addressed the package, and mailed it before—smiling with satisfaction—he strolled to the Emporium Barber Shop and Bath House. Now in no hurry, he luxuriated for an hour in a steaming-hot tub. He used up a whole bar of soap and told the attendant to throw his old clothes in the garbage.

In the barber shop portion of the establishment, he had his beard removed and his hair trimmed over the ears. He then dressed in a new dark-red shirt, black pants, the shotgun chaps, trail duster, and that Southwestern shootist's gray Stetson, ate dinner at the Colorado River House on the bank of the great waterway for which it was named. That night, he retired to a soft bed under a wooden ceiling for the first time in months.

Just before drifting off to sleep, he tallied his resources. He had given Chedan and Rose each five hundred dollars. Discounting what he'd spent today for food, clothes, trail supplies, and livery fees for his animals, that still left almost four thousand dollars, more than ample to fund his trip westward and to buy a nice ranch or perhaps start a fruit orchard after he arrived at the California coast. Smiling, he patted the gold-filled poke under his pillow, sighed once, and settled in for the night.

His good humor was still with him the next morning as he led Barbarossa and the horses onto the ferryboat to cross the river. When they reached the California shore, he mounted up and urged the mule along the stagecoach road westward. Presently, he sang into the hot, clear September morning air: "It rained all night the day I left, the weather, it was dry . . . the sun so hot, I froze to death . . ."

He burst into laughter for a moment before he said: "Damn you, Luther, you still got me doin' it!"

He didn't look back to see if Gibbs heard him, but kept riding, because he felt good. He had done the right thing. His conscience was clear, and he knew that up there in Heaven, Laurie approved.

THE END

BIBLIOGRAPHY

Brent, William, and Milarde Brent. 1962. *The Hell Hole: The Yuma Prison Story*. Yuma, Ariz: Southwest Printers.

Brewer, James W., Ron Foreman, and Southwest Parks And Monuments Association. 1993. *Jerome: Story of Mines, Men, and Money*. Tucson, Ariz.: Southwest Parks And Monuments Association.

John Mason Jeffrey. 1969. *Adobe and Iron : The Story of the Arizona Territorial Prison*. La Jolla, California: Prospect Avenue Press.

Smith, Nancy, and Jerome Historical Society. 1993. *Jerome: Tour Guide*. Jerome, AZ: Haven United Methodist Church.

Trafzer, Clifford E, and Steve George. 1980. *Prison Centennial, 1876-1976: A Pictorial History of the Arizona Territorial Prison at Yuma*. S.L.: Rio Colorado Press, Cop.

Yuma Territorial Prison State Historic Park Tourist Brochure, Arizona State Parks, Yuma, AZ

ABOUT THE AUTHOR

S. I. Soper was born in a remote valley in Washington state and lived in Oregon, California, Arizona, Texas, and Missouri, before returning to the shores of the Puget Sound. Soper, who worked for IBM for twenty-three years, came late to writing Western fiction, producing in the early years science fiction and fantasy novels. *Remittance Man* (2015) was Soper's first Western. Her first Circle V was *Hot Metal* (2019).